"You are always
making me angry."

Dane moved closer. "The next time I
do," he murmured, "why don't you
try kissing me? I guarantee it will shut
me up."

Bending his head, he moved his
mouth powerfully against her own,
parting her lips and invading them
with a hot sweetness.

A whirl of confused sensation began
taking over Pet's body. "Why did
you make me think I was so
incompetent?" she whispered
breathlessly.

"I couldn't tolerate anything but the
best from you because I knew you
could give it to me. You could always
give it to me."

There was the heady implication that
he was referring to more than her
work. As his hands glided slowly
down her shoulders, Pet struggled
for some semblance of control
before it was too late....

# JANET DAILEY

## one of the boys

*Harlequin Books*

TORONTO • LONDON • LOS ANGELES • AMSTERDAM
SYDNEY • HAMBURG • PARIS • STOCKHOLM • ATHENS • TOKYO

# CHAPTER ONE

TWO SMALL ROUND TABLES were shoved close together in the dimly lighted hotel lounge. There was hardly an inch of surface that wasn't covered with drinks, ashtrays, pretzel dishes and candle-burning globes. Almost a dozen chairs were crowded around the two tables, all of them occupied by men, except one.

Petra Wallis was the sole female in the group, but she was accustomed to that. At five foot nine she was as tall as most of them. Despite her khaki blouse and slacks of a mock-military fashion, there was nothing masculine about her. The very blandness of the unisex-designed clothes accented her slim willowy frame and served as a contrast to the long wheat-blond hair pulled away from her face and secured with a gold clasp at the back crown of her head. The length of it fell straight down her back in a shimmering silk curtain of gold.

Nature had blessed her with a flawless complexion and strong, classical features. Her jawline slanted cleanly to her pointed chin. Her mouth was wide with a sensually full lower lip, her nose straight with the faintest suggestion of an upward tilt at the tip. And her sea-green eyes possessed a naturally thick fringe of dark brown lashes.

"You should have put those mirror tiles on the ceiling, Charlie," someone suggested. "What do the wife and kids think about it, Charlie?" another person teased.

"Sandy loves it," Charlie insisted. "We can slip away for a weekend and have all the comforts of a motel room without the cost."

"It's all prepaid in the money you spent fixing the van," Lon Baxter stated from his chair next to Pet's, and reached for one of the glasses of beer on the table.

"Whoops! That's mine, Lon." Pet rescued her drink and put another glass in his hand. "This is yours."

"How can you tell?" He looked skeptically at the half-empty glass of beer she had substituted for the fuller one.

"Unless you've started wearing lipstick, this has to be mine." She laughingly showed him the peach-colored imprint on the rim of the glass.

"In this light I don't see how you can see anything." He groped in mock blindness, pretending to discover the bareness of her forearm. "Ah, what's this?" Setting his glass down, he took advantage of the fact that Pet was still holding hers. He turned in his chair to get closer to her while his other hand slid across her stomach, stopping on her rib cage just below the swelling curve of a breast.

"It may be dark, Lon," Pet smiled sweetly, "but I know exactly where your hands are. And if your left hand moves one more inch, you're going to get an elbow in the throat."

The warning was issued with deliberate casualness,

these next couple of weeks," she replied, not taking offense at the ribbing. "I'm not in the class of Ruby Gale, singer turned sex goddess. Lon won't even notice me after he's spent a day looking at her through his camera."

"Ruby Gale, the new Jersey Lily." Andy Turner, the fourth cameraman in the production crew, lifted his glass in an acidly cynical toast to the star of the television special they had come to tape.

Pet, Charlie, Andy, and Lon made up the team of four cameramen. She loathed the tag "cameraperson." The term seemed unnatural and a needless attempt to differentiate her sex, but she usually had to endure the label.

"She is fantastic!" One of the sound technicians spoke up in the singing star's defense. "Do you suppose she'd mind if I asked for her autograph? My wife and I have every one of her albums."

"I wouldn't ask her for anything until the special is all done," Andy advised. "She can be a royal bitch."

"You've worked with her before, haven't you?" someone asked.

"On an awards special a couple years ago," he admitted. "All she had was one song and an award to present, maybe five minutes of the entire show, but her incessant demands created total chaos. I've seen my share of temperamental performers, but Ruby Gale is the worst! This isn't any picnic we're on."

"Dane can handle her," a lighting technician insisted.

A grimness pulled at the corners of Pet's mouth. "Dane Kingston, the big man himself, is going to be

haired cameraman "—then it seems to me that she and Dane Kingston are perfectly mated."

"What do you have against Dane?" Andy laughed. "I wouldn't wish Ruby Gale on my mother-in-law, let alone someone like Dane. Besides, I always thought you women went for him. At least, my wife tells me he's quite a hunk of man. And I've always been convinced that she knows a good thing when she sees it—she did marry me."

The joking boast drew the expected round of guffaws and heckling from the group. The conversation could have easily been shifted to another topic, but the mere mention of Dane Kingston had set Pet's teeth on edge. She knew the tension wouldn't ease until she had talked out some of the animosity seething within, veiling it so the rest of the crew wouldn't guess how deeply it ran.

"I have no doubt Dane Kingston can be charming if he chooses." She tapped a long finger on her burning cigarette to knock off the ashes into the half-filled ashtray on the table.

"Let's hope he uses all his persuasive skills to charm our sexy star into performing without her usual temper tantrums," Andy suggested dryly. "Otherwise we'll be in for a long miserable time."

"Who says we won't with Dane Kingston?" Pet countered in a low, venom-filled voice.

"What did Dane Kingston ever do to you?" Charlie asked, subjecting her to his narrowed scrutiny. "I always heard he was an all-right guy."

"Dane Kingston?" She arched one pale brown eyebrow in mocking question, refusing to join the

was coming to see what was wrong, but he didn't let anybody know when he would arrive. One minute we were talking about him, and the next minute he was there. It was hot that day, really hot. The air conditioner was broken, wasn't it?" He glanced at Pet, a little vague on that point.

"It was making too much noise and they had to shut it off," she explained indifferently.

"That's right," he remembered. "Anyway, he walks in and what's the first thing he sees? Our Pet in a pair of white shorts and a sexy red tank top. It was between takes and she was getting lined up for the next shot. Evidently nobody thought to tell Dane that we had a woman on the camera crew, because he immediately assumed she was somebody's girl friend. He lost his temper and began chewing her out—and everyone else around her—for messing around with an expensive piece of equipment. Did you know who he was, Pet?" Lon paused in his story to ask.

"No. And I didn't particularly care," she retorted.

"That's for sure!" he laughed. "Nobody wanted to interrupt him to explain who she was, for fear he'd start yelling at them. So finally Pet just shouted at him to shut up. It got so quiet in that place you could have heard a flea scratch. Then Pet began reciting her résumé and wound up telling him that it was idiots like him who didn't know their rear end from a hole in the ground that were causing all the problems on the show, and suggested that he should take a long hike."

There was laughter, but it was generally subdued. The glances that were directed at her, for the most

"No, I'm going to say what I think. I don't like him, I've never liked him and I never will like him," she stated forcefully. "If he was here I'd say it to his face."

"Then maybe you should turn around," an icy voice suggested.

A cold chill ran down her spine. Pet turned her head slowly, her gaze stopping when it found the gold buckle of a belt around the trim waist of the man standing behind her chair. Traveling by inches, her gaze made the long climb up his muscled torso, past the set of huskily built shoulders, beyond the tanned column of his neck and the thinly drawn line of his mouth finally to reach the smoldering brown of his eyes.

Her pulse thundered in her ears, reacting to the male aggression of his presence. Pet's seated position intensified the impression that he was towering over her. Perhaps if she hadn't felt so threatened she would have acknowledged that he was a ruggedly attractive man. His dark hair was thick and full, inclined to curl while seeking its own style and order. The sheer force of his personality was enough to make her erect barriers of defense, rather than be absorbed by him.

"I believe there's an old saying that eavesdroppers never hear good about themselves, Mr. Kingston." Her voice was tight with the effort to oppose him.

The atmosphere around the two tables became so thick a knife could have sliced it. Someone coughed nervously while Lon shifted uneasily in the chair beside Pet. She continued to wage a silent battle of

"Sure."

"Good night."

The replies crowded on top of each other, drowning themselves out. Relief drifted through Pet now that Dane Kingston's unwelcome presence had been removed. She sipped at her beer, but it had grown flat and tepid.

"I feel as if I'm in a dormitory again, complete with curfew," she griped. "Do you suppose he's going to do a bed check and make sure we're all tucked in for the night?"

"Would you like me to tuck you in, Miss Wallis?" his voice came back to mock her.

She jerked around to find he was only a couple of steps away from the table, clearly close enough to have heard her ill-tempered complaint. She could have screamed in frustration, but managed to restrain her anger.

"No, thank you." She had to grit her teeth when she spoke.

"If you change your mind, let me know," Dane taunted deliberately, but his eyes were cold.

This time Pet watched him walk out of the lounge so she wouldn't put her foot in her mouth again. When she turned back to the table, the others eyed her askance, certain she had taken leave of her senses by being so antagonistic. There was a definite possibility that they were right.

"You're asking for trouble," Charlie mumured the warning.

"He rubs me the wrong way," Pet declared with a discouraged sigh.

"Good night, Lon." She turned to walk down her corridor, the silken straightness of her long blond hair swinging softly below her shoulder blades.

"Wait a minute, I'll walk with you." He hurried to catch up with her. Nearly the same height as Pet, Lon had the advantage of only an inch. As he curved an arm around her waist, his smile promised all sorts of pleasures.

"I can manage myself, Lon." She firmly removed his hand from her waist. "I don't need to be escorted. I won't get lost."

"I just wanted to be sure you got there safely." He looked affronted that she had taken his interest wrong.

"I'll tuck myself into bed. Good night, Lon," Pet repeated, and let her long legs carry her swiftly away from him.

He paused indecisively before he retreated to the fork in the corridor. Halfway down the hall, Pet reached her room. She had to wrestle with the doorknob before she could persuade the key to unlock the door.

The single room was small. The bed was a little wider than a single, covered with a quilted spread in a blue-flowered print. There was one blue green chair, the same color as the carpet, and a short built-in dresser with a mirror on the wall behind it. A proportionately small television was bolted to an extension of the dresser. The bathroom was about the only thing that was normal size.

Kicking off her flat shoes, Pet dropped her bag and the room key on the bed, and started to move

after ten. It would be a long day tomorrow, even if Dane Kingston had reminded her of it. She began unbuttoning her khaki blouse and tugging the hem loose from the waistband of her matching slacks.

A knock at the door stopped her action with only two buttons left to unfasten. "Who is it?" Pet called.

"Dane Kingston," was the muffled reply.

She didn't for one minute believe that it was the producer. Some members of the crew had a weird sense of humor. It was more than likely somebody's idea of a really funny practical joke. Irritation surged through her in a quick rush.

"Oh, go away!" she grumbled.

But the person simply knocked again. She had started to tell him she wasn't in the mood for jokes when she decided it would be much more fun to turn the tables on the gagster.

"I'm coming." She deliberately put an inviting lilt in her voice and discreetly buttoned a couple of buttons, but left the top ones undone to permit a provocative glimpse of the shadowy cleft between her breasts.

She sauntered to the door, not bothering with the safety chain as she turned the knob and pulled the door open. "Have you come to tuck me in, Dane?" she murmured sexily.

But it *was* Dane Kingston standing in the hallway!

"What do you want?" She let her exasperation show.

"I want to talk to you," he stated with a crispness that indicated the subject was not personal.

"You've talked to me. Now please leave. I want to get some sleep." She remembered the buttons and hurriedly began to fasten the strategic pair near her breasts. "As you pointed out, we have to be up early and work long hours tomorrow."

"This will only take a few minutes of your precious time, I promise you." Dane Kingston mocked her sudden show of concern for plenty of rest. "Are you going to invite me in? Or do we have this discussion in the hallway where anyone can overhear?"

The flat of his hand was still resting on the door. Pet guessed it would take only one push of that muscled arm to wrench it out of her hand. He could shove his way into her room if he wanted, and there was very little chance that she could prevent it.

"Aren't you worried that someone will see you come into my room at this hour of the night?" she taunted.

"No one that knows either of us. All the rooms for the crew are down the other corridor." There was a humorless curve to his mouth. "So you needn't worry that your reputation is going to be irretrievably damaged by this visit."

Damn! He made her look so foolish and unadult. "I was more concerned about yours," she retaliated, and spun away from the door, admitting him by moving away.

"What did you come to see me about?" She came

Pet was astounded by his suggestion—and angry. "What am I suppose to do on my off hours? Sit alone in my hotel room while the guys are in the bar having a good time? If that's your idea, you'd better think again," she informed him in no uncertain terms. "If I want to have a beer with the boys, I will."

"In case you haven't looked in a mirror lately—" he grabbed her by the elbow and turned her around to face the wall mirror "—you don't happen to be one of the boys!"

But it wasn't her own reflection that her turbulent sea-green eyes saw in the mirror. It was his, standing tall and dark beside her, overpoweringly masculine beside her willow-slim frame and wheat-tan hair. His innate virility aroused raw feelings of femininity in her. Pet tugged her elbow free of his hold and took a quick step away. She was used to feeling strong and independent no matter what man she was with, not weak at the knees.

"So what do you expect me to do—remain cloistered for the next couple of weeks or however long it takes to finish this special?" she demanded. "I'm not a nun! I like to laugh and socialize and—wait a minute!"

She turned on him roundly, a thought suddenly occurring to her. "Is there some significance to the fact that my room is in this corridor while the boys all have rooms in the other one? Was this your idea? Or is it just because this is a single?"

"When the hotel reservations were made, attention was paid to the fact that you are the only female

impact rocked him slightly. His large hands spanned her waist to steady both of them, the imprint of his fingers burning through the khaki material into her flesh.

Conscious of the masculine power of his thighs and the steel band of muscles flexing in his arms, Pet tried to collect her scattered wits and slip out of this accidental embrace, but her limbs wouldn't respond to the signals her brain sent out. She felt her heart skipping beats in sheer sexual attraction. Her mind reeled from the possibility that she could be physically attracted to the man.

"You're a stunning amazon." His low voice had a harsh edge to it. "Any normal, red-blooded American male—regardless of his age—would get ideas in his head if he spent a night alone in the same room with you. Don't tell me you aren't aware of that?"

The warmth of his breath fanned her face and hair like an intimate caress. Its potency was drugging. Fighting it, Pet abruptly turned her head to face him and make a retort. But in turning she discovered his head had been bent toward her, and in consequence her lips brushed the angle of his jaw. The resulting sensation was a shivery tingle that ran through her nerve ends, leaving them quivering for more. She twisted out of his arms as if she had been jolted by an electric prod.

"I'm quite aware of it. I didn't mean to imply that I wanted to share a room with one of—" That phrase "one of the boys" was becoming overused. "But I certainly don't think I have to be in an entirely different wing of the hotel from them."

would prefer a meatier explanation of his own was another question. Men were such gossips.

Turning, she saw Dane standing at the foot of the bed, watching her, his hands in the side pockets of his pants.

"Problems?" It was a one-word question with no apology for causing them.

"Nothing that I can't handle," Pet replied shortly.

His dark gaze slid to the phone, then back to her. "So you've decided not to take my advice."

"About socializing with the boys? No, I'm not taking it." With space between them she could think more clearly. She realized the way she had been manipulated, always in reaction to his statements and accusations, and she was irritated that she had allowed it to happen.

"You and I have differing viewpoints. In the bar tonight you thought I looked like a tramp sitting with all those men. For me there's safety in numbers. Before you came to my room I wouldn't have dreamed of accepting Lon's invitation to have breakfast with him alone. But I just did because I knew you would disapprove."

"That's a stupid reason." The corners of his mouth were indented with grimness.

"You bet it's a stupid reason!" Pet agreed. "I can't be friendly to just two or three of the guys. If I do, the rest will assume that I go for them, and that destroys the camaraderie I've struggled so hard to achieve. Why did you have to interfere? Nobody asked you to!"

"I don't need permission to interfere. This is my

"How old are you?" he demanded next.

"Twenty-six." She would be in September, which was only two months away. The extra year implied more experience.

"I top that by eight years. And I've seen happily married men make complete fools of themselves when they've been separated from their wives for a week. Why do you think Miss Gale and her singers and dancers are staying in a different hotel?"

"I...presumed it was more luxurious than this one." Pet shrugged a shoulder uncertainly.

"It is. More importantly, it keeps my production crew separated from her cast so there won't be any socializing after hours. If it had been at all practical, you would have been staying in a different hotel, too. Unfortunately, it wasn't." His irritation with that was in his tight-lipped expression. "You just remember what I told you—any trouble and you're out!"

On that threatening note he turned on his heel and let his long, swinging strides carry him to the door. Pet's hands curled into fists.

"You just remember what *I* told *you,*" she called after him, trying to assert her own independence, but it was too late. Dane was pulling the door shut behind him as he stepped out into the hall.

Frustrated and dejected, Pet sank onto the squeaking mattress of her bed. She flopped backward to stare at the ceiling and rest the back of her hand on her forehead. This had not been her finest hour, she realized. Nor was the situation likely to improve unless she learned to control her temper around Dane Kingston. He was her boss, for heaven's sake! The

"About a half a cup," Pet answered after glancing inside the pot. The waitress stopped at the table to take her order, Lon and the others having already eaten. "I'm running late, so I'd better settle for toast and orange juice."

"Would you refill the coffeepot?" Joe Wiles handed the empty thermal container to the waitress.

When the girl had left, Pet leaned back in her chair, blowing on the hot coffee to cool it. Over the rim of her cup her gaze swept her three table companions in an encompassing arc around the table. It was early in the morning, but their unnatural silence wasn't caused by sleepiness.

"Come on, guys." She sipped at the hot coffee. "Isn't someone going to ask me what Dane Kingston was doing in my room last night? Or are you going to sit there eaten up with curiosity?" she teased. She had it all thought out, her explanation carefully rehearsed.

"That's our Pet!" Joe Wiles shook his head and smiled wryly. "Straightforward and open."

"You said he lectured you?" Lon looked skeptical.

"Yes. He went off on the same old tangent," she declared with a mock grimace. "Only this time it wasn't about the way I dressed, but what I was doing. He didn't think it was ladylike to have a beer with you guys and he suggested I behave with a little more decorum befitting my sex. Can you imagine?" she laughed, and took another sip of coffee.

"From now on, we'll make sure you order sherry—a proper drink for a proper girl," Joe teased.

then on to Atlantic City to tape her opening night at the casino.''

"We're really going to be plugging New Jersey, aren't we?'' Lon remarked on a less than enthusiastic note.

"This is her home state. She was born and raised here in New Jersey,'' Claude reminded them. "These backdrops will all be fresh and new to a viewing audience that's seen Las Vegas casinos and Madison Square Garden or the Kennedy Center hundreds of times.''

"I agree,'' Pet nodded. "I think it's a good idea.''

"Spoken like a homegrown Jerseyite,'' Charlie teased. Which she was.

"Your New York nose is in the air again,'' she countered.

Joe didn't take part in their playful feud, choosing to stick to the original subject. "It's fitting to tape the special in New Jersey. After all, Ruby Gale has been tagged as the new, American-born Jersey Lily.''

"Lillie Langtry was the original Jersey Lily, wasn't she?'' Pet remembered. "But she was from England, I thought.''

"She was,'' Claude admitted. "Now we have an American version—if you believe the publicity.'' He paused to glance at his wristwatch. "You'd better drink your coffee, boys. It's getting late.''

Pet quickly downed her last bite of toast and joined the others in line at the cash register. Everyone took it for granted that she would pay for her own meal, including Pet. The situation with the crew seemed to be back to normal.

camera, which allowed him the ability to move around with the lighter-weight camera and provide shots from in back of the stage, from the side, or below the footlights.

The first order of business was erecting the platforms to elevate the fixed studio cameras to a degree higher than stage level. Working as a team, they pitched in to help each other erect the scaffolding for the platforms one at a time. Pet worked right beside the men, not shirking any of the heavier work because she was female.

While they were busy with their work, other members of the production team were busy with theirs. It was a chaos of activity with two dozen people, sometimes more, hustling around, shouting orders amid general conversations. A web of cables was spun over the floor to relay power and feed into the main controls in the long trailer outside.

As soon as the platforms were finished they brought in the studio cameras, disassembled and packed in their metal traveling cases. It wasn't easy for Pet to handle the bulky and heavy pieces, but she had learned little tricks over the years that enabled her to compensate for the lack of muscles. It never occurred to her to ask for help. She would have refused it if it was offered.

"Wallis, what do you think you're doing?" a voice barked behind her.

The suddenness of the demand forced Pet to ease the camera onto the platform floor after she had finally levered it a couple of inches off it. Still kneeling, she turned to look behind her. Dane Kingston

He waited at the base of the platform until Pet had moved stiffly out of Charlie's way so he could hoist the camera into place on the rotating head of its stand. As Pet went to help Charlie fasten it into place, Dane walked away. She glared after his set of broad shoulders.

"I've never considered myself superwoman," she muttered angrily. "And I've never asked for special treatment because I'm a woman. Damn him, anyway!"

Charlie's gaze flickered uncertainly over her. "You have to admit, Pet, the camera was a little heavier than you could handle."

"*Et tu, Brute,*" she retorted sarcastically, but Charlie didn't hear her as he turned to say something to Andy.

came and a few of the other crew, to talk shop. Pet listened, but spent most of her time eating to quiet the hunger pains in her stomach. When it was gone, she licked the sticky frosting from her fingers.

Tired of standing, but intrigued by a technical explanation Andy was making, Pet set her cup of coffee on top of the stage. With her hands to lever her, she vaulted onto the stage, swinging around to sit on the edge, her long legs dangling. Between sips of her coffee she listened to Andy and asked questions when she wanted something clarified.

She reached for the pack of cigarettes that she usually carried man-fashion in the breast pocket of her blouse. Too late, she remembered they had fallen out when she was assembling the camera.

"Can I bum a cigarette from somebody?" she asked. "I left mine on the platform."

"Here." Lon lighted one of his and handed it to her, the filtered end first.

"Thanks. Coffee without a cigarette is as incomplete as a steak without salt," Pet declared.

"Or a bed without a woman in it!" someone suggested, and everyone laughed in agreement, although Pet just smiled.

"Pet doesn't think so." Lon noticed her silence and began to tease.

"Nope. I have a teddy bear to snuggle up to at night," she joked. "It doesn't complain if I have a headache."

"Do you have headaches often?" Charlie asked with a laughing smile.

"Working with you guys, I have them all the

"I wasn't 'holding court,'" she insisted stiffly.

In one smooth motion he came a step closer and spanned her slender waist with his large hands. Instinctively Pet clasped his bare forearms with the intention of repelling his hands, but he was already lifting her off the stage and setting her feet on the few inches of floor left in front of him.

His hands stayed on her waist, as if he knew that the minute he took them away she would move out of his reach. She was forced to stay where she was, their tall bodies almost, but not quite, touching. His nearness was suffocating.

"Don't deny you were the center of attention," Dane stated, a muscle working in his hard jaw.

"Maybe when you walked up, but not before." Her gaze moved restlessly over his shirtfront, looking anywhere but into his implacable male features.

She watched the steady rise and fall of his chest, noticed the curling, golden brown hairs peeping out through the V opening made by an unbuttoned collar, and saw the brawny muscles beneath the shirt sleeves over his upper arms. It was a disturbing observation of his utter masculinity.

"They were clustered around you like bees around honey." His voice was low, but that didn't lessen its cutting edge.

"That isn't true," Pet denied. "They'd gathered around the stage because it gave them something to lean against."

"They leaned against the stage rather than sit in those seats out there," Dane mocked. "In case you

"They work with you, but that doesn't mean it never crosses their mind to wonder what you'd be like as a lover. Men tend to think along those lines," he said. "Women probably do, too, but they're reluctant to admit it even to themselves."

"I don't think very many women think like that," she replied huskily.

"No? You've never wondered what it would be like if—for example—I made love to you?" Dane queried, tilting his head to one side.

"No." Pet rejected such a notion with a rushed answer and pushed at his forearms. "Now let me go. I have to get to work. I can't keep standing around here talking to you."

"Or the boys might start to think I was in your room last night for a reason other than the one you told them?" he suggested complacently.

"They wouldn't." But she turned to look toward the middle platform where Charlie and the others had gone to finish assembling the camera. As she watched them, Andy glanced over his shoulder toward the stage. The object of his attention was obviously her and Dane.

"They would enjoy thinking it," Dane insisted dryly.

"Well, I wouldn't!" Angered that he had placed her in another awkward situation, Pet wrenched out of his hands with a violent twist. "So just stay away from me from now on!" With a quick pivot she whirled away from him, her long braid flying out behind her and nearly slapping his face.

Anger gave her a surplus of energy. She burned a

She never fully recovered her sense of humor. By the time they broke for lunch, Pet had succeeded in pushing the disturbing incident to the back of her mind. The others had either forgotten or were careful not to bring it up.

In the afternoon, the impression of chaos was increased when the cast of entertainers arrived to practice their songs and dance routines. To an outsider, it had to look as though no one knew what was going on, but it was all very well organized.

Wearing her headset to communicate with the control booth in the semitrailer, Pet was checking out her camera to make certain it was functioning properly and transmitting a clear picture to the monitors in the control booth. Invariably when a sophisticated and sensitive piece of equipment such as this television camera was transported any distance, something needed adjustment. Although generally the adjustments were minor, they could be time-consuming, which was why a day was set aside more or less for the sole purpose of assembling and checking out the equipment, including the spare camera. Barnes was the name of the technician in the control booth with whom Pet and her co-cameramen were working.

"She's here. She just walked in the door." It was Lon's voice that came over Pet's headset. "Wow! She's sexier in person, if that's possible."

"You mean Ruby Gale? Where is she?" Charlie questioned.

Pet had the feeling she was listening in on a party line as the headset hummed with the intercommunication of the cameramen. The star of the television

a kiss. In the entertainment business, kissing was as much a part of greeting as a handshake.

"Do you see the way she's cuddling up to Dane?" Charlie murmured. His voice coming over her earphones was an unneeded verification of the scene Pet was witnessing.

"I wish she'd press against me like that," said Lon, and imitated the sound of a growling tiger.

"Dane's certainly enjoying it," Andy observed dryly.

"There would have to be something drastically wrong with him if he didn't," Lon retorted. "Hey, you're awfully quiet, Pet. Isn't there any comment you want to make?"

It took her a second to find her voice. "About what?" With the pencil-thin microphone directly in front of her lips, it didn't take much above a whisper to make herself heard. "She's an absolutely gorgeous woman, but you can't expect me to be turned on about her the way you guys are."

Ruby Gale was very beautiful. Pet could see that now as the redhead half turned toward the audience seats. Her features were sultry and exotic. Her dark eyebrows were perfectly arched, winging to her temple. Full, sensuous lips appeared always silently inviting some forbidden pleasure. Although Pet was too far away actually to see the color of her eyes, she remembered from the photographs of Ruby Gale that they were a startling peacock-blue.

"A word of warning, fellas," Andy inserted. "She has a temper to match the color of her hair."

"I don't care," Lon declared. "All I know is that

dinner every other sentence contained some reference to the star of the television special. It seemed everyone had some anecdote to relate or gossip to add. At the conclusion of her meal, Pet stayed at the table to have coffee with the guys.

When the exodus began toward the lounge, she decided that she couldn't endure another minute of Ruby Gale and opted to return to her room. No one seemed to notice that she wasn't coming with them, which was rather bruising to her ego.

Perhaps that was why she didn't notice Dane Kingston standing near the exit of the restaurant until she was almost level with him. Her steps faltered for a brief instant.

"Good evening," she murmured, and would have walked on.

"Aren't you going into the lounge with the others?" His dark eyes moved over her with lazy knowledge.

"Not tonight. It's been a long day and I'm tired," she explained because she didn't want him to think her decision had been based on his admonition not to socialize with the men in the crew.

"It never crossed my mind that you were heeding my advice," Dane assured her. "But I can't say that you look tired, either."

Pet took a deep breath and released it in an exasperated sigh. "The truth is, Mr. Kingston, that I've become bored with the subject of Ruby Gale. It's all I've heard for the last several hours."

"You don't like playing second fiddle, is that it?" he mocked.

"What? No champagne and caviar?" There was a certain acidity to her murmured taunt.

"That's being saved to celebrate the completion of the special," Dane responded easily.

"How nice. Enjoy your evening," she said, and hurried on her way before he could stop her again.

It was too early to go to bed. After twenty minutes in the small hotel room the walls began to close in on her. Jamming her writing pad and paperback book in her large shoulder bag, Pet left the room and went out of the hotel through a side door leading to the pool area.

There were two families with children swimming in the pool, but few of the deck chairs were occupied. Pet chose one with a small wrought-iron table beside it. It was nearly a full hour before sundown on this warm summer evening—not that it mattered, since the pool area was lighted.

Shedding her blazer, Pet settled into the deck chair and got out her writing pad. She had barely written "Dear Rudy" when a shadow was cast across the paper. She looked up to find Joe Wiles's wide bulk standing beside her chair.

"Writing love letters?" he smiled.

"It's to my brother. He's in the coast guard. Right now he's stationed in Texas, along the Gulf Coast," she explained. "Are you taking an evening stroll?"

"Yeah, I'm taking my nightly constitutional before turning in," he grinned, and pulled up a chair to sit beside her. "Do you have any other brothers or sisters?"

"An older brother, Hugh. He lives in Connecticut,

Joe?'' she offered, and reached in her purse to get change for the drink machine standing against the exterior wall of the hotel.

''No, thanks,'' he refused, and pressed a hand against his rotund stomach. ''Those carbonated beverages give me heartburn.''

There was a definite golden cast to the western sky. Pet noticed it when she walked back to her chair after getting the cold can of soda. For a fleeting second she allowed herself to wonder whether Dane and Ruby were admiring the sunset together in her suite.

''Why do you suppose Dane Kingston has never married, Joe?'' she asked with absent curiosity. ''Or has he been?''

''Not that I know about,'' he answered her last question first. ''Could be his reason is the same as yours—never met the right girl. He's certainly had more than his share of beautiful women hanging on his arm over the years.''

''And probably hopping into his bed, too,'' Pet added on a note of disgust. ''I'll bet no one has ever said yes to him, because he's too bossy and pushy. A woman can't tolerate that for long.''

Joe shook his head in disagreement. ''In this life you have to go after what you want. Nobody is going to hand it to you.' I admire the way Dane never lets anything stand in the way of what he wants. He knows what it is and goes for it. I like that. There are very few men like him in this world.''

''That's heartening,'' Pet murmured dryly.

''I'm not going to argue with you about him,'' Joe declared, and pushed to his feet. ''I'd better finish

# CHAPTER FOUR

THE ORCHESTRA WAS POSITIONED to the rear of the stage, the pianist testing a few quick chords to loosen his tension. The dancers in their practice leotards were posed around Ruby Gale, standing at front center stage. Beyond them the backup vocal group was fanned out.

This was a practice session, a dry run before tomorrow's dress rehearsal and the following night's concert. Each one of the songs and dance routines would be performed so camera angles could be corrected and the lighting adjusted.

The cameras were warmed up. Everyone on stage was waiting for the cue from Claude, the floor director. Dane Kingston was in the control booth in the van parked outside. It was his instructions and directions that were coming over Pet's headset.

"Camera two, we'll be opening with you," he informed Pet. "I want a close-up shot of Miss Gale, widening on my order. We'll be coming to you next, camera three. All right, we've been through this number twice already. I want the tape rolling on this one."

Pet nibbled at her lower lip, tension building as she rechecked her focus. She knew the procedure. The practice tape would be made and reviewed later that

"Hold the shot, two. We're on you," Dane advised. "When she moves stage left, go with her, Wallis." Pet tried, not very successfully, as Dane's angry voice informed her, "You're letting her get behind a dancer. Three, take it on the turn—quick! You blew that shot, Wallis."

She gritted her teeth, not convinced the fault had been entirely hers. She suspected the dancer had been out of position, although no one was ever precisely where he was supposed to be. Either way, there wasn't time to dwell on who had been in error. She had to be in position for her next shot.

Meanwhile, she listened to Dane heaping praise on Andy. "Great shot, one." The even pitch of his voice didn't change, although a level of amusement entered it. "I didn't know you had it in you, Turner. You'd better make certain you can do that again." Then, crisply, "You're off center, Wallis. I can't come to you until you have Ruby in the middle. You've got it!"

Concentrating, Pet followed the star through her next sequence of steps and its accompanying song lyrics. Her coverage was flawless. But she didn't receive the deserved praise from the control booth; Dane's attention was occupied elsewhere.

"Baxter, you're in three's picture. Duck behind the reed section," he ordered the cameraman on stage with the handheld camera. "Okay, three, it's yours."

As the song drew to an end, Pet's was the last shot. It was to be a close-up on the star while she belted out the last line, then opening to full length and finally

tuated with swearwords, as if vulgarity somehow emphasized his enthusiasm.

"Let's clean up the language!" Dane snapped. "You're forgetting, Baxter, that there's a lady listening."

"A lady?" Lon questioned, then hooted, "You mean Pet?"

"That's exactly who I mean!" was Dane's angry and silencing retort.

In the past, Pet had always turned a deaf ear to that kind of language rather than inhibit her male coworkers. If they weren't able to talk freely, she had always felt she would be driving a wedge between herself and them. So she didn't welcome this interference from Dane Kingston.

"Don't worry about it, fellas," she said into her microphone. "I have special earphones that automatically censor any words that might shock my virgin ears. All I hear is a confusing set of bleeps."

"Miss Wallis—" Dane's voice came low and threatening over the headset "—I give the orders around here. It's of little interest to me whether you would be offended or not. As long as I'm running this show, there isn't going to be any more of that kind of language around a woman. Is that clear?"

"Perfectly." She ground the response through her teeth, crimsoning at his sharp reproof.

"Now that we all understand one another, let's get ready for the next number. Ruby is doing a solo on stage. You shouldn't have any trouble this time, Wallis, in making sure no one else blocks the star out of your shot," he suggested sarcastically.

"It's a good thing Claude suggested a fifteen-minute break," Lon remarked. "We came very close to seeing that temper Andy has been telling us our star has. You should have heard some of the things she said to that poor dancer who forgot the routine! If Dane thought my language was out of line, he should have heard some of the words Ruby Gale used."

Pet wished he hadn't brought that earlier matter up. As if he realized what he had said, Lon glanced at her, noting her strained and downcast expression. A rueful grimace twisted his mouth.

"I guess I do owe you an apology, Pet. Some of the things I said were really off color. I forget sometimes that you're not one of the boys. I'm sorry," he offered.

"Forget it. I have." She crushed out the tasteless cigarette.

"I agree with you, Lon," Charlie inserted. "Dane was right to remind us that Pet's a woman. A lot of times we don't show her the respect that we should."

"Listen, I've never asked for any special treatment from you guys," she reminded them.

"If you think I'm going to open a door for you, you're crazy," Lon joked, trying to make Pet see the situation with a little humor.

"Sorry, I'm a little touchy. It's been a rotten day what with Kingston constantly harping on me," Pet explained with a genuine effort to contain her irritation. "I can't seem to do anything right."

"Maybe you're trying too hard," Charlie suggested.

Oriental look. Her jade silk blouse buttoned up the front with a mandarin collar and a hand-embroidered water lily on the left side. The top was complemented by a pair of mother-of-pearl slacks. It was usually a morale-boosting outfit that enhanced her proud carriage, but she didn't feel any better when she studied her reflection in the mirror.

Sighing, Pet left her hotel room. Too on edge to have dinner yet, she decided to stop in the lounge and have a relaxing before-dinner cocktail with the boys. Her plans went awry when she walked into the dimly lighted bar and didn't see Charlie, Andy or any of the regular group. At a table near the bar she noticed Claude, Joe Wiles, Dane Kingston and the audio man, Greg Coopster, all seated together.

She started to leave, then decided to have a quiet drink by herself; after all, that was the reason she had come into the lounge. When Joe spoke and the others glanced around, Pet just nodded. She didn't approach their table as she made her way to a secluded booth in the corner. The barmaid came to take her order.

"A glass of sherry, please." Why on earth had she ordered that, Pet wondered when the miniskirted girl had walked away. Was she trying to prove what a "proper" lady she was?

Reaching for the pack of cigarettes in her purse, she shook one out. The lighter flamed with a quick snap. As she lifted the light to the cigarette, a shadow blocked what little light reached the corner booth. Her hand began to shake even before she looked to see who was there.

Because she had already guessed it was Dane

her, Pet stared at the glass of sherry sitting on the cocktail napkin. She didn't even notice the ashes building up on the end of her cigarette or the gray blue smoke curling from its tip. His gaze was making a slow inspection of her profile; she could feel it as certainly as if he were touching her.

"Do you want to please me?" The drawled question suggested intimacy lightly spiced with a vague curiosity.

His implication sent her imagination off on a forbidden tangent. If he could affect her this deeply just by sitting next to her and hinting at familiarity, how would she feel if he made love to her? Her heart knocked against her ribs.

"I couldn't care less," she lied, impatient with herself for being physically disturbed by him. It gave false credence to her statement. She reached for the sherry glass. "Why don't you go away and leave me alone? I was doing fine before you came along."

"A woman alone in a bar is a target for any man who walks in. You can't sit here by yourself," Dane insisted, gently this time.

But it only increased his attraction and made her all the more determined to resist it. "Did it ever occur to you that maybe I wanted to be picked up by some—traveling salesman?" she challenged angrily.

His gaze narrowed to bore relentlessly all the way to her soul. "Is that what you want?"

Bravado failed her, but she managed to hold on to her poise. "All I wanted was a quiet drink before dinner and a chance to relax. If you're finally satisfied, will you please leave?"

"I'm not going to let you sit here by yourself.

of her elbow even though she was standing and didn't
require his assistance anymore.

His fingers transmitted the natural warmth generated by his body and sent it spreading up her arm. It
made her flesh tingle quite pleasurably. Briefly, she
was tempted by the prospect of spending more time
in his company until she remembered the tapes they
would be viewing. She had endured enough of his
criticism for one day.

"Is that an order?" she questioned, turning to pick
up her drink and thus forcing him to release her arm.

"No, you aren't required to attend." Something
flickered in his look—displeasure, perhaps.

"Then I respectfully decline," Pet replied with
faint mockery. "Excuse me."

Pausing long enough to inform the barmaid that
she was taking her drink into the restaurant, she
entered the dining room through the connecting door
to the lounge. She did eat alone. It wasn't until the
waiter brought her coffee that any of the crew arrived. Pet could have joined them, but there wasn't
any point.

Too restless to return to her room, she wasn't in
the mood for the kind of shoptalk the group would
be having in the lounge, so she wandered outside to
stroll around the pool area and watch the sunset from
a lounge chair. Reentering the hotel, she stopped by
the small gift shop and newsstand to look around.

Ruby Gale's face stared at her from the cover of a
movie magazine. Curious, Pet leafed through the
pages to find the article about the star. Several
photographs of Ruby accompanied the write-up. One

staff inside, emptying ashtrays and carrying away the coffee cups. She quickened her steps to catch up with the heavyset man.

"How did the meeting go?" she asked.

The carpeted hallway had muffled her footsteps. Joe's balding head turned with a jerk at her question.

"You startled me," he accused without anger.

"Sorry. Did you make many changes after you saw the tapes?" She walked with him. For the time being, they were both going in the same direction.

"Surprisingly, very few, and most of those were minor," he replied. "Audio has some problems that they have to correct, but Dane was satisfied with the video. He's going to experiment with the switcher tomorrow, try for some different effects on the solo numbers."

"But it looked good?" Pet persisted. It didn't seem possible that Dane was as satisfied with the results as Joe implied.

"Of course. Did you think it wouldn't?" His smile was a little confused. "It will be even better tomorrow. Having everyone in costume will really make a difference in the finished product."

"Yes, I know it will," she agreed absently.

"What time does the dining room close?" Joe glanced at his watch. "I haven't eaten yet and I'm starved."

"I think they stop serving at eleven."

"I'd better hurry." He raised an eyebrow. "I'd like at least to wash and change my shirt before I eat."

They reached the point where the corridor

frowned. "I thought the meeting finished only a little while ago. I just met Joe in the hall."

"It just broke up," he agreed, and inserted the key in the lock again. "And no, I haven't had dinner."

She studied his bent head and the curling thickness of his dark brown hair, and her hands itched to run their fingers through his hair and feel those vigorous strands beneath her palms. She was shaken by the force of that unbidden desire. She clenched her hands tightly around her bag in case she unconsciously gave in to it.

"You have to eat." She tried to concentrate on the subject. "It isn't healthy to skip meals."

With a deft twist of his wrist he turned the key in the lock and pushed her door open. "Don't worry. I'll have room service send a sandwich or something up to the suite," he promised smoothly as he turned to face her.

"The suite?" she repeated. Separated from him by only a few feet, she noticed the shadows along his cheeks. The lights overhead were bright, clearly illuminating his rugged features. The darkness was obviously caused by a fast-growing beard.

Her thoughts returned to the implication of his statement. "Then you're on your way to Miss Gale's hotel."

"Yes," he nodded, and moved out of her doorway.

"At this hour?" She said exactly what was on her mind and instantly regretted it. "I'm sorry, it's really none of my business."

"It isn't," Dane agreed, but he regarded her with lazy indulgence rather than anger. "After viewing the

girl before her first kiss when she saw the room key in his hand. Her fingers loosened their death grip on her handbag to reach for it but they weren't given the chance to take it from him, because the key was forgotten entirely as he lowered his mouth onto hers, blotting out everything.

A splintering shock held her motionless until the warm taste of his mouth melted her stiffness. She responded easily to the persuasive ardor of his kiss, a glow spreading through her veins. There was even pleasure in the light scrape of his beard against her soft skin. Desire grew within her to deepen the kiss, to realize the potential delirium that it promised.

Something cold and flat slipped inside her blouse where the top set of buttons was unfastened. Her skin shrank from the contact, but couldn't elude it. It took her a dazed second to identify the object as a metal key. The discovery was followed close on the heels by the realization that Dane's fingers were guiding it inside the left undercup of her bra.

Before she could protest his flagrantly intimate action, Dane was lifting his head and withdrawing his hand from inside her blouse. She tried to look indignant, but she wasn't very successful—the smoldering gleam in his dark eyes told her so.

As if to prove how completely within his spell she was, he circled her left breast with his large hand. The possession was light, in no way forcing her to endure his caress, while claiming his right to do so.

"Now you've finally pleased me, Pet," he murmured in a voice that nearly melted her knees. "Get a good night's sleep, hmm?"

While she was still trying to surface, he was mov-

# CHAPTER FIVE

THE NEXT MORNING it was work as usual, with a meeting scheduled first thing to go over the few changes. Other than a vague smile and nod in her direction, Dane paid no more attention to Pet than to any other member of the crew. She tried to tell herself that she wasn't disappointed, that she hadn't really expected anything different.

In an effort to show she was heart-whole and carefree, Pet threw herself into her job and worked to establish the old camaraderie with the boys. She had kissed men before without it meaning anything and forgotten it the next day. She could do so again.

It was later in the morning before they were ready to actually begin taping the dress rehearsal. The production crew had plenty to do to keep busy while the cast spent their time in Makeup and Wardrobe.

All the performers were finally on stage for the opening number except for the star, Ruby Gale. When she walked out to take her position, Pet gave an audible gasp at the gown the redhead was wearing. At first glance it didn't appear to have any sides. She stared to see why it didn't flap open and that was when she noticed the flesh-colored netting at the sides.

"I said cut the chatter, Wallis!" Dane barked in her ear.

It didn't matter that he was out in the large van where she couldn't see him. A mental image of him sprang into her mind—his mouth hard and tight-lipped and his dark eyes blazing. Pet was stung by the injustice of being singled out by his barbed tongue.

"Why pick on me?" she griped to herself, but forgot to push the highly sensitive microphone away from her lips. "I'm just about the only one whose eyes haven't popped out of his head."

Since she hadn't intended her comment to be heard by anyone, she visibly jerked when Dane answered her question. "That is exactly the reason. The others can't help themselves, but you can, Wallis. So straighten up!"

"Yes, sir! Anything you say, *sir!*" She masked her angry defiance with exaggerated obedience that left no one in doubt of her temper.

Any question about what last night's kiss might have meant no longer existed. As far as Pet was concerned, the meaning was clear: it had been nothing more than a passing whim. Dane was going to be hard and rough on her today to make sure she understood that and didn't get any ideas. The message was loud and clear. Pet was neither deaf nor stupid. After all, she hadn't really thought she could successfully compete with that red-haired sex goddess on stage. And she hadn't forgotten that Dane had been with Ruby Gale after he had left her.

It was another ten minutes before the floor direc-tor told the performers to take their positions on

Silently Pet seethed at this preferential treatment for the star. Nothing remotely resembling a critical word was ever directed at Ruby Gale. Why couldn't Dane snap at her the way he did everyone else, she thought angrily. In his eyes Ruby Gale could do no wrong, while Pet couldn't seem to do anything right. She felt raw, suffering from a thousand needling remarks, oversensitized by a barrage of pinpricks.

She had the closing shot on another production number. "Hold that frame, camera two," Dane's voice advised sternly in her ear. "Hold it. Hold it!" Impatience inched into his tone and scraped at her nerves. "Okay, stop tape."

At the statement, Pet immediately closed her eyes and lowered her chin in wary relief. Her long blond ponytail swung forward to brush the top of her left shoulder. Releasing her grip on the control handles of the camera, she wiped her sweaty palms on the legs of her faded denims. She straightened to glance across the rows of seats to Andy's camera position and he gave her a crooked smile and a thumbs-up signal.

"We made it through that one," his voice murmured through her earphones.

Before she could reply, Dane's voice came over the public-address system. "Good job, gang. I think we've earned a twenty-minute break."

The richly resonant pitch of his voice vibrated over Pet. "Ah, a voice from above," Charlie joked, and lifted his hands in mock awe.

"Regardless of what he thinks, he isn't related to God Almighty," Pet muttered, assuming that Dane

"What got into you, Pet?" Charlie came up to stand beside her. The smile on his face seemed to be there in spite of his better judgment. It was as if he admired her for talking back while he thought she was crazy for doing so.

Lon was there, shaking his head. "You really believe in flying in the face of danger, don't you?"

"I just want him off my back," she grumbled, and swore under her breath when she tried to take a drink of the scalding black coffee and burned her tongue.

The explosion of a door being forcefully slammed shut thundered through the cavernous theater and echoed in shock waves. A quick glance over her shoulder saw Dane striding toward them. Squaring around, Pet kept her back to him and hooked a thumb through the belt loop of her jeans, trying to adopt an attitude of nonchalance while studying the black liquid in her cup.

"I'm afraid you're in for it, Pet," Andy murmured, glancing at her over the rim of his drink.

With an exaggerated blink of her eyes, she pretended she didn't care. The skin along the back of her neck prickled a warning. Out of her side vision she saw Dane stop on her right, but she wouldn't look at him.

"You didn't really think you were going to get by with that, did you?" Dane sounded remarkably calm as he made the low challenge.

There wasn't an adequate reply she could make to that, so she didn't try. To cover her silence, she started to raise the cup of coffee to her mouth, but Dane reached out to take it from her.

in her veins was hotly sweet, searing her with a buoyancy that convinced her she was floating on a cloud. She stopped resisting and began kissing him back, her hunger matching his appetite.

Before her hands could begin their final, submissive curve around his middle, Dane was drawing away. There was a disturbed roughness to his breathing and the smoldering darkness of passion in his eyes. Yet the clearest impression Pet had was the scattered cheers and applause of those around them.

The crew regarded the kiss as a huge joke, thinking that Dane had deftly turned the tables on her. And it was true. The heat of embarrassment rushed into her face, staining her cheeks scarlet. Pet couldn't remember ever blushing in her life, but she had never made such a fool of herself. For a few seconds she had forgotten all that had gone before the kiss.

She lowered her gaze to the tanned hollow of his throat, his arms still containing her within their circle.

"Why did you do that?" she asked huskily. Had she really deserved this kind of humiliation?

Dane crooked a finger under her chin and forced her to look at him before he would answer her question. "It seemed the most effective way of shutting up a smart mouth." The lazy glint in his dark eyes seemed to hold only amusement at her discomfort. "And if you do it again, the next time I'll bite off your nasty tongue." He tipped his head back and to one side, as if to get a better angle of her face. "Truce?"

Before she could answer, someone called to him

Dressing for the taping that evening, Pet chose the dressier biscuit-colored slacks and a peach crepe-de-chine blouse and wrapped a brown braided rope belt around her waist. Her everyday work garb was too casual to wear in front of the public, and a dress or skirt was out of the question since she still had to climb off and on the platform.

The audience began arriving at the Garden State Arts Center half an hour before the performance was scheduled to begin. Perched on her platform in the center aisle, Pet became the cynosure of many eyes that had nothing better to do than look around while waiting for the show to start. It was amusing to listen to some of the comments.

A young brunette about her own age pointed Pet out to her date. "Look, there's a woman operating that camera."

Her date had a typical chauvinistic reply. "She's probably only a helper."

A few stopped to ask questions, most of them concerned about when the show would be seen on television. "I don't know the air date," was Pet's stock answer. "Probably in the fall or winter."

Sometimes they asked where she had learned to operate the camera. "I went to college and took courses in it."

In a way, the most difficult question to answer was why she wanted to be a cameraman. "It's what I always wanted to do," rarely satisfied them.

As the time drew closer to nine o'clock, Dane's voice came over her headset. She had barely seen him at all since yesterday's episode. The few times she had, he had been in conversation with someone else

"Gotcha, boss."

Precisely at nine the curtain went up. Right from the opening number the first half of the show went without a hitch. The mistakes by both crew and performers were so few and minor they were practically nonexistent. It seemed that all the rehearsing, the countless takes, the endless criticisms had all paid off to achieve near perfection.

Ruby Gale's performance had been electric, charged by the applauding audience. She was sexy, stunning, scintillating, alive as Pet had never seen her before. Everything flowed with such magic that when intermission arrived Pet couldn't help wondering what would happen when the clock struck twelve and the coach became a pumpkin again. Would the spell wear off?

"Excuse me, miss." An elderly man was standing beside her platform. Pet had noticed him before since he was sitting in one of the aisle seats near her position.

She shifted the mike wand of her headset away from her lips. "Yes?" She thought he probably wanted direction to the men's room. She supposed she could always ask Andy or Charlie.

"I've been watching you and I just wanted to say that you're a very beautiful woman," he said, smiling quite benignly. "You belong in front of the camera instead of behind it."

"Thank you." Her smile was wide and wholly natural.

"I know you're busy, but I just wanted to tell you that." He nodded in a gesture of apology and turned to go back to his seat.

"Are you driving back to the hotel with me?" Charlie called to her from across the seats.

"Yeah! But I left my bag in the van," she explained. "I'll run out and get it now. Wait for me!"

The seventy-foot-long semitrailer had seemed the safest place to leave her bag during the taping. She couldn't have kept it with her on the platform since it could have been stolen too easily. Nor had it seemed wise to leave it backstage with so many people coming and going all the time.

As she walked in front of the stage, a woman stepped out from behind the curtains. Pet had seen her before. She was usually a part of Ruby Gale's personal entourage. Pet suspected she was a secretary or something.

"Excuse me," the woman requested Pet's attention with an uplifted finger. "Could you tell me where I could find Mr. Kingston?"

"I—" Pet glanced around the theater "—haven't seen him. He might still be in the trailer outside. I'm on my way out there. Shall I send him in?"

The woman considered that, then said, "Could you give him a message?"

"Sure," Pet nodded.

"Miss Gale is leaving now for her hotel. She wanted to remind him about the party she's having in her suite tonight. Would you mention it to him? Miss Gale is most anxious that he should come," the woman added.

"I'll remind him," Pet promised.

"Hurry up, Pet!" Charlie shouted.

With a quick wave to acknowledge that she had heard him, she hurried out through a side exit to

rubbed his forehead. Both his sound and his action made it plain he wasn't overjoyed by the message.

Pet watched him, feeling a little glad that he didn't look happy about going. "She also said Miss Gale was most anxious for you to come," she added.

"I don't have any choice," Dane said wryly. "It's more or less obligatory on both sides. Ruby has invited some of the local dignitaries and the press over for drinks. It's good public relations—and good publicity. It's good for her, and for this television special of mine," he explained. "It's one of those business affairs masquerading as a social event."

Pet wasn't exactly sure why he was telling her this. It wasn't really any of her business what this party was for or why he felt obligated to attend. But the fact that he had made her feel...well, a little important.

"That's often the case in the entertainment business, I've heard," she offered in sympathy.

"Have you ever been to one of these parties?" Dane asked, tipping his head to one side and smiling faintly.

"Heavens, no!" she laughed.

"Why don't you come with me tonight?" he suggested. "Then you'll always know what you're not missing."

For a minute she thought he was serious, then she wasn't sure. "You don't want me along." She shook her head, her long blond hair swinging loose about her shoulders, and started to climb the last steps to the van door.

"I wouldn't have asked if I didn't want you come

"I'll tell him to leave without you, that you'll be with me. The gang will really be confused then," he grinned. "I'll meet you here."

"Okay," she agreed.

When she opened the trailer door, Dane had disappeared into the semidarkness. Pet didn't understand this spell he had cast over her. One minute she was infuriated with him, and in the next he could have her melting in his arms. It didn't make sense, but she wasn't sure if it had to.

Her bag was right where she had left it, tucked under the bench seat inside the door. She glanced once at the multitude of television monitors across the control panel, the screens glassy and gray, all the little lights out. Behind the panel, out of sight behind the partition, was the sophisticated computer that controlled everything and turned the semitrailer van into a portable television studio, complete with all the latest electronic gear. Pet shuddered to think how much it cost, or how wealthy that made Dane, since he owned it.

to her skin, heating her flesh with an awareness of him.

Under the sweep of her lashes she slid him a look out of the corner of her eye. His roughly sculpted profile caught at her breath, disrupting its evenness. She was struck again by his height, something she didn't notice about most men since they generally weren't so much taller than she was.

As if he felt her eyes upon him, Dane's gaze swept down on her in a lazy caress that upset her heartbeat. She quivered all over inside with the desire to have him make love to her. It was faintly shocking to be so completely aroused by just a look. In delightful agitation she averted her gaze to the door, her ivory-smooth features hinting at this inner disturbance through the fluttering of her lashes and the tilting of her chin.

Dane's hand applied slight pressure on her hipbone as if he wanted to pull her closer. "You look very lovely," he murmured, and she guessed the reassurance was intended to eradicate any nervousness about her appearance. But how could she explain that a Dior gown wouldn't change the physical reaction erupting from his nearness?

"Thank you." It was a breathy answer, barely audible.

With excellent timing, the door was opened to the suite by the same woman who had given Pet the message for Dane. The polite smile she gave Dane faltered when she saw Pet with him. "Good evening, Mr. Kingston. Miss Gale will be so glad you could come."

"I thought hotel suites like this existed only in Hollywood movies," she commented.

"It's horrendous, isn't it?" he agreed, keeping his voice low, too. "You should see the main bedroom. It has a round bed with a red velvet canopy draped into a rose design. I think I prefer mirrors to staring at giant red roses above my head."

A sick feeling weighted Pet's stomach. Was he speaking from experience? Of course he was. She was angry with herself for even questioning it. How else would he have known about the bed unless he'd lain in it? Only a completely naive fool would believe he had only been testing the mattress for firmness. And she wasn't naive. She had always suspected—known—that he and Ruby were lovers, so why had she accepted his invitation to this party? The answer was so plainly simple. She had a fatal fascination for this sexy, exciting man who could enrage or arouse her by turns.

This inability to resist him made her feel spineless. She took another sip of champagne, wildly hoping the effervescent spirits would temporarily stiffen her backbone. The constricting muscles in her throat rejected it with a tiny choking cough.

"I'm surprised the champagne isn't pink," she managed at last, her long fingers delicately covering her lips.

"Ruby probably didn't think of it." A smile twitched the corners of Dane's mouth as his gaze ran interestedly over her face, a little aloof. "I told you this would be an experience. You find it distasteful, don't you?"

canes—sugar and spice wrapped up in glitter and se-
quins. It's called packaging the product.''

"I suppose that's true," Pet conceded with a trace
of his cynicism.

"You haven't been formally introduced to the
'product,' have you?" Dane remembered, and closed
a hand on her elbow. "We'd better correct that omission before Ruby starts throwing real poisonous
darts instead of invisible ones.''

Following the direction of his callously amused
glance, Pet saw their hostess through a gap in the
cluster of guests. Her long hair was about her white
shoulders in a mass of titian curls. The daringly cut
spangled gown was the same peacock-blue shade as
her eyes—eyes that glittered with impatience and irritation whenever they rested on Dane, which was
often.

When Dane and Pet had weaved their way through
the crowd to the star's side, Ruby Gale gave Dane
one of her radiantly provocative smiles. "I wondered
when you were going to show up, darling," she chided him playfully for his tardiness, and curved a
scarlet-nailed hand along the back of his neck when
he bent to greet her with a kiss.

Their lips clung together a few seconds longer than
the length of a merely casual kiss. Pet was prepared
for the violent surge of rage that shook her. She
stood motionless, her face frozen into blankness,
while the three men Ruby had been speaking to ex-
changed knowing glances and raised eyebrows.

When Dane lifted his head, the star wiped the
traces of lipstick from his mouth with her fingers.

Wallis. She's been operating the number-two camera.''

"The center one?" Now the star's gaze became sharp, slicing Pet into unimportant pieces. "You actually have a woman in sole charge of a camera? I didn't realize you were so liberated in your views, Dane. You've never exhibited that tendency before."

"Haven't I? Maybe you just never noticed," he suggested, turning aside the comment.

"Are you his token female, Miss Wallis?" the star inquired archly. In explanation to the other men, Ruby Gale defended her question. "With all these new laws nowadays about hiring women for traditionally male jobs, it's almost mandatory for an employer to hire a woman if she applies for a position. Me, I'm not in favor at all of this new equality for women. I love being the weaker sex, and dominated by a big, strong man." Her glance at Dane made it obvious who that "big, strong man" was.

Pet seethed with jealousy and the sensation of betrayal by one of her own kind. What Ruby Gale was insinuating was insulting and demeaning to her. Worse, the three men with their glasses of champagne and lascivious looks were nodding agreement with Ruby Gale's remarks.

"I can assure you that I wasn't forced to hire Miss Wallis," Dane inserted lazily. "Her sex had nothing to do with her employment. I doubt if it was even taken into consideration by anyone in the company."

His support didn't bring the reassurance that it should have. Instead, one of the younger men—a reporter by the cynical look of him—gave Pet an

"I am," she admitted, since flattery also implied exaggeration.

"Is that why you brought Miss Wallis to the party? As a reward for all her work?" Ruby questioned, and rose on tiptoe to kiss his cheek. "How sweet of you, darling! You really are very thoughtful."

The conclusion Ruby had reached sent Pet's mind racing. Was that the explanation for this unexpected invitation? Was she to regard her attendance at this party as a bonus for a job well done? She had liked it better when she believed it was just a friendly invitation.

"I'm not certain if Pet would agree with you, Ruby." Dane commented, and sent a roguish glance in her direction. "I think she's convinced I'm a cross between an ogre and a tyrant."

"You neglected to mention an interfering busybody," Pet reminded him smoothly.

"So I did," he agreed, and lifted his champagne glass in wry acknowledgement of the omission.

"What's this all about?" Ruby glanced from one to the other, suspicion shimmering in her hard blue eyes.

"A minor rebellion in the ranks against authority." Dane dismissed their previous skirmishes with an indifferent shrug of a shoulder and sipped at his wine. "I neglected to tell you how sensational you were this evening, Ruby. You had the audience in the palm of your beautiful hand all the time."

Diverted by his compliment, the redhead beamed, "Thank you, darling."

"Hear, hear," one of the men murmured in agree-

Pet had the distinct impression that Ruby Gale had given him permission to escort her. It would have proved more bolstering to her self-esteem if the star had resented Dane's accompanying her. This way the woman obviously didn't regard her as representing a serious threat.

The three men introduced themselves, but Pet didn't make an effort to remember their names. Dane chatted with them a few minutes, then took Pet by the arm to wander to another group. The procedure was repeated several times, and Pet realized that Dane was doing his own brand of circulating, advertising his product and making himself known to those who were important. A necessary part of any business was socializing.

But she had a great deal of difficulty relaxing in his company. She could talk quite naturally with others, yet could manage only a stiff nod or some stilted reply when Dane addressed a remark to her. Tension began drumming at her temples, demanding a respite from the constant strain of his presence.

A particularly garrulous guest had trapped Dane into a conversation about the merits of the present television programming, and Pet took the opportunity to touch his arm lightly to briefly claim his attention.

"Excuse me, I'm going to freshen my lipstick. I'll only be a few moments," she murmured as his gaze wandered over her mouth to assess the need.

Without waiting for his permission, Pet moved away. The brunette secretary whom Dane had addressed as Clancy showed her where the ladies'

second before she remembered he was one of the three who had been talking to Ruby Gale when she and Dane had joined them. At the time she had decided he was a reporter.

"Yes, it is." She continued to stand straight and tall.

"Petra Wallis, isn't it?" he remembered her name.

"Either you have an excellent memory or else you know everyone else here," Pet replied with a wry look over the rim of her champagne glass.

"It's a combination," he admitted. "I know most of the people who are here, remembering names is part of my trade, and a man would he a fool to forget yours."

He smiled for the first time without some inner cynicism. In his late thirties, he wasn't really an un-attractive man without that expression of bored superiority. Plain brown hair and shrewd brown eyes went with his unassuming features. As his gaze made a thorough study of her, it didn't contain the sug-gestive stripping quality that he had subjected her to before. Pet didn't feel any of the initial hostility he had generated in their earlier meeting.

"I know you've probably forgotten. The name is Nick Brewster." He wasn't offended that she had.

"You're with the newspaper, right?" She wasn't sure if she had been told or if it was only a guess.

"Yeah, I'm doing a feature article on the 'Tiger Lily' for the entertainment section. I'll probably send it around—syndicate it to a few other papers." He shrugged to hide the boasting tone, then studied her

of becoming aloof, he chided her, "Everyone knows that the two of them are having an affair. They aren't trying to hide it, even if he did drag you here."

"I wouldn't presume to discuss Mr. Kingston's private life with you, even if I were privy to any of that kind of information—which I'm not," she retorted. "I'm an employee, nothing more."

"Such loyalty!" he mocked her, his gaze sliding sideways. "It should be rewarded, Mr. Kingston. But I forgot," he pretended as Pet turned to find Dane standing near her elbow, "this invitation to the party was by way of a reward."

"You should ask who's being rewarded, Mr. Brewster." Dane smiled pleasantly and laced his fingers through hers. "Maybe the pleasure of Miss Wallis's company is my compensation for a week of hard work and long hours."

"I wouldn't be surprised," the reporter laughed. "Some people can have their cake and eat it, too."

"Then you won't mind if I don't share. Excuse us."

Dane led Pet away. The smile faded from his expression, if it had ever really been there at all, and his dark gaze was sharp as it examined her. "I'm sorry. I hope Brewster didn't subject you to too much of his dirty digging."

"He didn't." She was curt as she pulled her hand free from him. She disliked being used as a red herring. "Not that it matters. I'm not in the habit of airing other people's dirty linen, even if I had possession of it—which I don't."

"We must," he said firmly, and sent an aloofly apologetic glance to the others for having interrupted them. Smoothly, he bent forward to kiss an artfully rouged cheek.

"I suppose you must," Ruby sighed, and let her glittering blue eyes wander to Pet. "After all, Miss Wallis is a working girl." The tone seemed to relegate Pet to an inferior class. "Call me tomorrow, darling. But not too early."

"It probably won't be until the afternoon. I'll be busy in the morning," Dane replied.

"Good evening, Miss Gale," Pet inserted so she wouldn't be ignored or treated as if she weren't there.

"Good evening, Miss Wallis." The phrase was returned, but most indifferently.

Then Dane's hand was on her waist, guiding her away toward the door. When the stocky secretary appeared Dane dismissed her with a brisk, "We can find our own way out. Good night, Clancy."

"Good night, Mr. Kingston."

across her, the sensitive nerve ends in her breast aware of every rippling outline of his muscles beneath the silken material of his shirt sleeve.

"What's bothering you, Pet?" His voice was low and taut with command.

Her head turned away from the door to bring him into her side vision, but she didn't look at him. She was conscious of the hard cast of his features, the determined grimness in the set of his jaw, and the harshness of his thin mouth.

"Nothing's bothering me," she insisted in cool dismissal.

"Something is," Dane persisted, not relaxing his hold so she could open the door. "And I don't believe it had anything to do with that reporter Brewster anymore. You were acting like this before he cornered you."

"I don't know what you're talking about," Pet lied in a weary breath. "I'm tired, so will you please let go of my hand? I'd like to go to my room and get some rest."

For a long second she didn't think Dane was going to release her. A barrage of suffocating sensations closed in on her. The air was warmly thick with the male scent unique to him, spiced with a whiff of his after-shave lotion. Under his muscled arm her heart was drumming its panic, while her flesh quivered ecstatically beneath his touch.

Then the talon-hard grip of her wrist was loosened and the restricting band of his arm was removed, setting her free. She sensed the impatience and irritation in his action, just as if he knew he could have ob-

with a low snarl. "It was a lousy evening and we both know it."

"All right, it was!" Pet agreed sharply, reacting to his anger out of self-defense. She forgot about the key in her need to get inside the room and shut the door on him.

Before she could succeed, his outstretched arm had stiffened to keep the door jammed open. "I want to know why," he demanded.

The hollow wood door seemed an inadequate shield against the man filling its frame and bracing it open with an arm. Yet Pet stood partially behind it, taking advantage of whatever protection it offered. The silken material of his beige shirt was stretched across his male physique, outlining his muscled torso and intimidating her with the contained strength that lay beneath it.

"Maybe I don't like being patronized!" she flared. "Did that ever occur to you?"

He shoved the door all the way open, pushing her backward as if her weight against it were no more of a deterrent than a feather. His long stride carried him past the door.

"You're going to explain that remark!" he snapped, stopping before she felt threatened enough to retreat in the face of his advance.

With a backward push of his hand he sent the door swinging shut, although it didn't latch, only fell closed in its frame. His hands were on his hips, his stance challenging. Pet found the strength to confront him with all the many wounds to her pride she had endured that night.

"For starters, I didn't appreciate those absurdly

"Then listen to reason," he demanded, and brought his face close to hers, his tanned features etched with fierce determination and suppressed anger. "You must have some small idea of how much money I have wrapped up in this special. Do you think that I chose this production crew at random? Every member I personally handpicked, because I wanted the best! And that includes you! I've reviewed everything you've done. I knew I was borrowing trouble by bringing a single woman on location—a *beautiful* single woman, I might add. But trouble or not, I'd have the best. That's why you're here, so what I told Ruby wasn't a lie."

His explanation made sense, but Pet couldn't relate it to the way he'd treated her these past few days. She eyed him warily, distrusting her ability to sort fact from fiction where he was concerned. He simply had too much influence over her ability to reason.

"Is that what made you angry, Pet?" he questioned in a gentler tone as his gaze roamed over her face, then paused to linger on her mouth and watch it form an answer.

"You're always making me angry." That was easy to admit. "You're always saying something to irritate me."

"The next time I do," he murmured, moving closer, "why don't you try kissing me? I guarantee it will shut me up."

Bending his head, he took her lips. Pet stood very still, inwardly shaking with the desire to put her arms around him, but she permitted her hands to go no farther than his chest, resting lightly on his shirt and

"That damned party was the last place I wanted to go tonight," he muttered, lifting his head to satisfy himself that she did look kissed and aroused. "But I had to go. It was as compulsory for me to attend as it was for Ruby to give it. And I knew the crew would be having a celebration of their own. If you weren't with me, you'd be with them."

"So you were just keeping me out of trouble again." Hurt, she flattened her hands against his chest, resisting, yet aware of the heavy beat of his heart.

"I wasn't looking after you." Dane shook his head wryly. "I was looking after me. You get into a man's blood, Pet. I thought I had a chance of enduring that insufferable chatter if you were with me, but it all went sour within minutes after we arrived, and I couldn't understand why. I thought you wanted to be with me as much as I wanted to be with you."

"Did you really?" She wanted to believe him, but she was afraid to. The doubt glistened in her green eyes.

"Can you doubt it?" he demanded, and crushed her lips beneath his mouth, devouring them in a rapacious assault of passion that left her breathless and dazed.

The pressure of the hand at the small of her back was fiercely possessive. She was hardly conscious of his other hand moving to stroke her hair. His fingers found the gold barrette that secured the top and sides in a single clasp at the crown. With a deft snap he unfastened it to let the silken length tumble free, and a half-muffled groan rippled from his throat as he tunneled his hand beneath the golden mass.

movement cleaved their lips apart, but there wasn't any way they could untangle their hands from inside each other's clothes. In cold shock, Pet stared at Lon and the handful of other crew members clustered around her door.

Dane recovered a shade quicker than she did, withdrawing his hand from under her blouse to let it rest reassuringly on her arm. His action drew her glance, and she shuddered at the grimness in his features and the accusing silence from her co-workers.

"The door was open," someone mumbled in an attempt at an apology.

"Yeah," Lon agreed, swaying belligerently in the opening. "We wanted to invite you to our party, but you were having a little private one of your own, weren't you, Pet?"

The color that had receded from her cheeks came flooding back. She looked away from the door, pushing at the rumpled length of hair near her ear. Vaguely she was conscious of someone urging Lon to come away from the door, then Dane was letting her go to button his shirt.

"*All* the parties are over, boys," he stressed in a tired voice. "It's time we all called it a night. We have to tear down and pack the equipment first thing in the morning."

A few embarrassed mumbles of agreement followed his statement. The quiet shuffling of feet was a vast contrast to their exuberant, revel-rousing arrival as the men retreated down the hallway.

"Pet?" His quiet use of her name lifted her head. Dane was near the open door, half-turned to study her.

jaw. She arched her neck to allow access to the sensitive skin along its curve, and the mouth nibbled a slow path to the base of her throat and returned up the other side.

A soft, sensuously contented sound came from her throat, inviting that pair of masculine lips back to hers to urge a further response. Arms that had been flung above her head in sleep were lifted to find the one who was causing all these wonderful sensations. Her languorous hands encountered a muscled set of wide shoulders encased in some smooth material that allowed her to feel the contoured outline of his hard flesh.

A forearm rested on the mattress alongside her to position him above her while his other hand caressed the bare skin near the curve of her opposite shoulder. It was all so beautiful, so enchanted—like a dream that had come to life. Dane felt so solid and real, his thick springing hair curling around her fingers as she curved them to the back of his neck.

Gradually it dawned on her that the dream was real. It was all the better when she slowly lifted her lashes and saw that rugged face poised an inch above her own. Finding him sitting on her bed and kissing her awake was much too pleasant a surprise for Pet to be shocked. Her initial reaction was curiosity. She shifted her head on the pillow to get a better look at him, her gaze wandering to the lazy half curve of his mouth and her hands sliding from his back to his arms.

"How did you get in here?" she murmured with a flicker of a curious frown.

"I forgot to return your key last night. Evidently I

"You'd better let me up." She nudged him with her hands in a gentle reproof to move. "I still have to get dressed."

"I have a better idea," Dane murmured, settling more firmly into place. "Instead of you getting up, why don't I climb into bed?"

"No!" Her refusal was too quick and too weak, because she had never been exposed to a sweeter temptation in her life.

"Why not?" It wasn't a question to which he expected an answer as his mouth traveled onto her lips as soft as a wind song, and the probing point of his tongue traced their outline.

His fingers slid the strap of her nightdress off her shoulders. It immediately loosened the dark lace of the gown's bodice, allowing his hand to slide inside and cup her breast. Pet breathed in sharply in an unconscious and searing response. With masterful ease Dane explored and caressed its sensitive point into pebble hardness.

It took a concerted effort to turn her mouth away from his tantalizing kiss. "Dane, I have to go to work," she insisted tremulously.

"Have you forgotten?" He laughed softly against her throat, confident and male. "I'm the boss. I'm giving you the morning off."

"A special assignment?" She resented the use of his authority.

"If you want to call it that." He missed the hint of bitterness in her tone. "I want you, Pet. I want to make love to you." An element of urgency entered the rough pressure of his mouth against her cheek,

"Yes, I'm awake," she answered back, her voice growing steadier in its volume.

"When you didn't show up for breakfast, I thought I'd better check," Lon replied in explanation of his presence. "What did you do? Oversleep?"

"Yes," Pet admitted. "Thanks for checking."

"I've brought you some coffee."

Which meant she had to open the door. She threw an anxious glance over her shoulder at Dane. His mouth was compressed in a tight, hard line, a grimly resigned expression on his features. She pushed her tousled hair away from her ear and walked reluctantly to the door, holding the front of her robe shut.

Behind her, Dane made no attempt to conceal himself from view. Lon saw him standing at the end of the bed the instant she opened the door and his gaze flashed over Pet in silent condemnation.

"I should have known why you overslept," he jeered.

"It isn't like that at all," Pet denied his conclusion in a weary voice.

"Like you, I also noticed she wasn't around," Dane inserted. "I brought her coffee, too. One cup." He lifted a Styrofoam cup to show the camerman. "So you can lift your imagination out of the gutter."

"Listen, you may be Dane Kingston, the big man around here—" Lon stabbed an angry finger in the air adopting a belligerent stance "—but you want to crawl in bed with her the same as I do!"

Pet shivered at the cold rage that flashed across Dane's face. "I'm going to forget you said that, Baxter. Now get out!" he snapped.

"Like hell!" Lon took a step forward.

# CHAPTER EIGHT

PET DRESSED in a hurry, taking time only to put some lipstick on and tie a green scarf into a knot that gathered the hair at the nape of her neck. Leaving the room, she mentally braced herself for Lon's inquisition, but he wasn't in the lobby when she reached it.

Dane was, however, looking out a window in a relaxed stance. But when he turned to meet her, she realized he wasn't relaxed at all. He was a coiled spring, all poised to unleash that contained energy.

"Where's Lon?" Pet glanced around, knowing she wouldn't find him, but the action provided her with a few seconds to readjust her defenses.

The dark impatience of his eyes swept her. "I imagine he's at the center by now."

"He said he'd wait for me," she reminded him.

"I changed his mind." Dane stated what she had already guessed.

"I fully hope that you intend to give me a ride, otherwise I'll be without transportation to work." There was the right inflection of challenging humor in her cool voice to make it a casual remark. Her raw nerves hadn't betrayed her.

"I don't need to be reminded that you prefer work to a morning in bed with me. You've already made

"You're mistaken," she denied calmly while a hot pain twisted her stomach. "I'm not interested in anything she has."

"And you think she has me?" he mocked, the corners of his mouth deepening in derision.

"Haven't you heard?" Pet cast him a false look of surprise. "It's common knowledge."

"And you believe it." Dane challenged with a hard glance.

"Do you deny it?" she countered.

"I didn't think I had to." On that half-savage note, he pressed his foot on the accelerator to send the Jaguar shooting past the slower car in front of them. It was an awesome display of power and agility that Pet found somehow characteristic of him.

"I'm sure you didn't. There are probably plenty of women who would be glad to go to bed with you without caring who else you might be sleeping with, but I'm not one of them," Pet stated when the burst of speed was over.

"And what was last night? A momentary lapse of moral principles?" Dane mocked derisively.

"I didn't go to bed with you." It was a moot point but the only defense she had.

"No, but you were damned well willing!" he reminded her brutally. "Or are you forgetting that you were undressing me!"

Her cheeks flamed with the memory of it. "I'm trying very hard to forget that."

But Dane didn't pay attention to her tightly worded reply. "In another fifteen minutes the boys would

When they reached the turn to the center, Dane took the corner fast, the low-slung sports car hugging the curb as it whipped around it with a squeal of tires. He braked abruptly near a side entrance where men were entering and exiting to get all the gear loaded.

As Pet reached for the door handle, Dane said, "You can tell the boys I'm docking your pay for being late this morning. I know you won't want them to think I'm showing you any favoritism." There was a sarcastic curve to his cruelly thin mouth.

"Thanks." She matched his tone as she climbed out of the car and slammed the door.

She had one foot on the curb when he leaned across the seat to add, "By the way, I haven't slept with Ruby since a green-eyed blonde invited me into her room to tuck her in. So you might give me credit for some degree of constancy," he accused harshly, and gunned the motor before accelerating away.

Momentarily stunned, Pet couldn't persuade her legs to move. She stared after the fast-moving car and its driver. What exactly had he said? She knew the words, but what did they mean? *No, no,* she admonished herself, *don't get your hopes up. Don't be a fool. You were right—it's just a physical thing, and the last complication you need in your life is an involvement with your boss.*

Heads turned when she entered the building. Self-conscious, she paused, aware of the hushing of voices. Squaring her shoulders, she walked briskly forward to the partially dismantled studio camera at the number-two position.

"We wondered if you were going to show up for

minded her, not for the first time. "We'll probably get lost before we get there."

"I doubt it," Pet offered dryly.

"I'd like to know whose harebrained idea this was," he muttered. "Location shots in New Jersey of all places!"

"New Jersey is more than a corridor you have to pass through between New York and Pennsylvania." Her state pride insisted that she couldn't let that remark go unchallenged. "I know that's all most people see as they zoom through on their way someplace else. No one wants to believe we have swamp, marshes, miles of beach, farms, forests and lakes. If they can't see it from the highway, it isn't there."

"This must have been your idea, then," Charlie declared with a laughing glance.

"Why do you think it's called the Garden State?" she retorted, ignoring his remark.

"Because it has 'gardens' of concrete," he joked. "That's all I've ever seen. Hey!" He smiled broadly. "I just thought of something. Ruby Gale is the lily of the Garden State. That's a pretty good slogan, isn't it? Why don't you mention that to Dane?"

"Why me?" Pet stiffened because she knew precisely why. Charlie believed she was on very friendly terms with Dane. She could have been, but she wasn't going to go into a long, detailed explanation of why she wasn't anymore. "It was your idea. You tell him."

"He'd be more apt to listen to you, wouldn't he?" Charlie probed for information.

"I seriously doubt it," she replied with assumed indifference.

There was no work to be done on their arrival. All the location shots would be set up the following morning, which left Pet and the small crew free to wander through the village on the late and lazy summer afternoon.

Pet would have been content to stroll along the streets and browse through the curio tables, but typically the men were soon bored with such passive entertainment. Someone produced a Frisbee, and before Pet knew what was happening she was engaged in a lively game of catch in a park square. It was boisterous fun, leaping high to catch the soaring disk and trying difficult catches behind the back or under the leg. It was exactly the kind of distraction her tense nerves needed.

The Frisbee came sailing in her direction, but just as she got set to catch it, the wind caught it to change its trajectory. The disk drifted backward, and Pet realized at the last minute that it was going to be high and to her right. She turned to make a diving leap for it and rammed right into a solid object.

Her not inconsiderable height and weight staggered Dane backward, but she managed to keep them both upright. Pet wasn't sure if it was the impact or the shock of finding herself in his arms that stole the breath from her lungs. She stayed there, unable to breathe for several seconds while her fingers were spread across his chest and her head was thrown back as she stared into his vitally male face.

Her hair had long ago escaped the confining knot of the scarf and was a windblown mass of wheat gold. Dane's hands were on her waist, holding her

"Thank you," she murmured awkwardly, and turned away. He couldn't know how much he had contributed to the color in her hotly flushed cheeks.

Taking a few quick steps, she sailed the Frisbee back to Charlie with a flick of her wrist. But it took a nose dive short of its target, and a shirtless Charlie came trotting forward to retrieve it.

"You're welcome to join us if you like, Miss Gale," Charlie invited, puffing slightly behind his wide grin.

"No, thank you." The redhead refused with a laughing recoil at the thought. She sent a coy glance at Dane and slipped a hand under his arm. "Dane would hate it if I looked as hot and disheveled as she does," she declared with a pointed glance at Pet.

Pet had been conscious of her appearance before, but that remark made her doubly uncomfortable. Which was just what the star wanted. Ruby looked as if she had just stepped out of an advertisement for sports clothes in her snow-white skirt and candy-pink blouse.

Rather than stay where the contrast in their appearance was so marked, Pet decided to switch with one of the others. "Let me have the shady side for a while, Rick." If she looked hot and disheveled, there wasn't any point in quitting. Besides, she didn't want to give Ruby Gale the satisfaction of knowing she made her feel self-conscious and unattractive.

After she had traded places with the sound man, she saw Dane and Ruby strolling away arm in arm. It hurt, because she wanted to be the one walking with Dane. If she had stayed in bed, it was entirely possible she could have been. She shook her head to rid it of that tantalizing thought.

on top of her head, secured on the sides with combs
and on top with a leather hair poke. With it loose
there was too much risk of catching a strand on a
part of the camera or between the pad and her shoulder, which often resulted in a sudden and painful
yank on her scalp when she moved or altered position.

Dane's gaze made an absent inspection of her hair-
style as he approached her, but it was the only recog-
nition of her sex that he made. His rugged features
were impassive, all his attention focused on the
business at hand. The fluttering of her pulse revealed
that she had not achieved his objectivity.

"Ready, Wallis?" His gaze centered on her for a
piercing second, long enough to see her positive nod.
When he turned away, virile charm leaped from the
smile he gave Ruby. "We can begin whenever you
say, Ruby."

If he had wanted to make clear the difference in his
attitude toward the two women, he had succeeded.
Pet felt almost chilled by his callous lack of interest.
Instead of being enchanted by the warmth Dane had
shown the star, Ruby Gale appeared anything but
pleased.

"What's *she* doing here?" she demanded, and
pointed a scarlet fingernail at Pet.

"She's operating the camera, of course," Dane
smiled.

"How can I possibly flirt with the camera the way
you want when I'm looking at her?" Ruby protested
with an angry gesture of her hands.

"Flirt with the lens, my love, and think of the male

As she shifted the camera off her shoulder to set it on the ground, Charlie moved over to help her. His eyebrows were raised in a sympathetic look. She managed a grim smile and a supposedly uncaring shrug, then began unstrapping the bulky packs from around her waist.

"It will take us a few minutes, I'm afraid, to switch the equipment," Dane explained to Ruby. "Why don't you relax and have another cup of coffee while you're waiting? There's no need for you to stand around."

"Are you sure you don't mind, Dane, about using a camera*man*?" the redhead persisted. "I'd hate to think I was interfering in your job."

"If I thought she was irreplacable, I would argue with you. So you needn't be concerned that you've upset me," he assured her.

As soon as Pet had removed all the gear and given it to Charlie, she slipped self-consciously away from the location set. She was aware that Dane had observed her departure without comment. By getting rid of her, he had averted a scene and a possible delay. It had been the sensible thing to do, she knew that, but it did sting to be rejected so readily.

"We wrapped it up about twenty minutes ago. Too many shadows." He leaned a hand on the rough bark of the tree trunk and let his gaze roam the surroundings. "It's peaceful here."

"Yes," she agreed. Her glance slid away before it actually met his. "Charlie will be waiting for me, then."

"He was packing the equipment up when I left. I told him I'd find you and send you along to his van." Dane continued to study her with disconcerting directness.

"He'd probably like some help. I'd better go." But she didn't want to leave.

"Pet, about this morning, it wasn't by choice that I ordered you off the set." His dark eyes were grave as they searched her face, waiting for her response.

"I know." She looked across the green grass to the village center, liking its quaintness. "You did it because you had to keep Ruby happy for the sake of the production."

"Yes." He reached out to take hold of her forearm and force her to look at him. "But who's going to keep *me* happy? Will you?"

Unable to answer, Pet could only gaze into the masculine face with its tanned skin drawn tight over angular features. But the longing to be the one who could keep him happy was written in her jade eyes. She heard his sharply indrawn breath, then his mouth was coming down to crush hers.

His arm hooked her waist to haul her against his length. The contact with the taut columns of his thighs and hard flatness of his stomach made her

closer to her lips. His breath was warm and moist, caressing on its own. "I keep seeing it this way—the way it was yesterday morning, a tawny, rumpled cloud on your pillow. I never should have used that key, or else I should have thrown Baxter out."

"Why didn't you tell me you weren't...involved with Ruby anymore?" Her voice throbbed as her arms curved around his middle.

"Why didn't you ask me?" Dane countered. "God, I thought I'd made it obvious. Do you actually believe I would invite another woman to a party given by my mistress if she and I were still lovers?"

"You...you could have been having your cake and eating it, too." Pet recalled the phrase the reporter had used. It had sounded so plausible at the time.

"I could have." He tugged at a handful of hair to force her head back. His gaze seemed to stab deeply into her. "But I'm not the type. What are you doubting now? I can see it in your eyes. Very expressive eyes they are, too."

"I was just wondering how you knew about the rose canopy above her bed," Pet admitted, because the question would plague her until she knew. "You said you hadn't slept with her lately, but—"

"I haven't." Irritation put a harsh edge on his voice. "All entertainers seem to have little eccentricities; hers happens to be going over new arrangements while sitting in bed. In order to have a discussion of them, it seems logical to join her on the bed. I suppose I could have pulled a chair up, but I don't happen to be bashful or easily embarrassed."

pered on a tiny sob. "I'm unsure of how I feel, what I think, what I do. Every ounce of sense I have tells me I shouldn't want you, but I do."

With a muffled groan he pulled her forward against the hard warmth of his mouth. The hand at the nape of her neck began stroking it softly and sensuously, sending shivers tingling down her spine. A faint hungry sound rolled from her throat as she arched against him, surrendering to this wild joy that flamed from his kiss.

When she wound her arms around his neck, his mouth parted in an irresistible invitation to deepen the kiss, and Pet accepted it eagerly. In direct response, his hand flattened convulsively on her hips, shaping her more firmly to him to give her potent evidence of his need, and she trembled uncontrollably.

Abruptly Dane dragged his mouth from hers, the hand at the back of her head applying pressure to bury her face against his neck while shudders racked his torso. She could feel the hard, uneven thud of his heart. The rate of her own pulse would have rivaled the speed of his car. Happiness was such a fragile thing. Its beauty filled her eyes with tears and swelled her heart to the point of bursting. How could she ever contemplate denying this ecstasy that she was a kiss away from discovering?

Her hands spread across the broad muscularity of his back to hold him closer while her lips began exploring his throat, savoring the taste of his skin and absorbing the heat of his flesh. In a slow, roundabout way she reached his ear, her tongue delighting in the shape of it. A raw sound of desire came from

leave now for Atlantic City. There are a few details I have to iron out with the management at the casino. Then I have to be back here for the taping tomorrow. We aren't going to have any time to be together."

"I see." She didn't ask if she could go with him. If Dane had wanted her along, he would have invited her. He had to know she would accept.

"I still have a company to run, so my schedule is going to be like this until this damned special is done," he said, revealing his impatience and irritation at the circumstances, which offered some consolation. "I want you to understand that isn't the way I want it. I don't want you getting any crazy notions in your head that because I'm not with you, I don't want to be. No more of that imagination of yours working overtime about rose canopies and being patronized or whatever ridiculous molehill you can make into a mountain."

"No more." Pet shook her head in promise.

"There's another thing you'd better know. I don't give a damn what the crew thinks about us. You can keep on trying to be one of the boys if you want. But if I get a chance to touch you or kiss you, don't you dare shy away from me because one of them might be watching," Dane warned. "I'll be discreet. There won't be any passionate clinches in front of them, but I'm not going to guard my every look and action. If they want to accuse you of receiving special treatment, you can tell them for me that you damned well *are* special! Any objections?"

"None. Half of them think we've already slept together anyway," she admitted, a little thrilled by his possessiveness.

aren't going back, not even if I have to replace you. You're going to stay with the crew. You aren't going back until we all go home. I know I'll be working all the time and maybe I'll only get to see you five—ten minutes, half an hour at a time. But I'll know you're there and if I get the chance to be with you, I will."

Keeping her at a distance, he kissed her, his mouth clinging to her lips for an enchanting instant before he lifted his head. The sweet torment of longing made his expression bleak and grim. Pet wanted to smooth away the hardness in his face with her hand, but he wouldn't let her touch him, as if not trusting his reaction.

"You said before that you were unsure," Dane said tightly. "Maybe you can appreciate the way I feel. The times I've been with you haven't been among my more rational moments. It's like being trapped between two battling weather fronts—one hot and the other cold. I never know which it's going to be with you."

"You pick a lot of the fights yourself." Pet wasn't that submissive that she would accept full responsibility for their arguments. He had been at fault, too. "You shouldn't say things you know will irritate me."

"Maybe I have." He granted that it was possible without admitting it. "From now on, understand the pressure I'm under. If I'm sharp with you, be tolerant...at least until this taping is done. I'd sell my soul to have it finished right now." Then Dane laughed, a wry sound. "Some say I made a pact with the devil when I signed the contract with Ruby."

*and nothing must happen to her.* But Pet didn't let that voice speak.

ALTHOUGH PET WASN'T PRESENT during the next morning's taping, she gathered from what Charlie had intimated at lunch that it wasn't going well. Ruby Gale was being difficult and demanding, and Dane wasn't satisfied with the results they were getting. Only the crew knew of his displeasure, from what Pet could tell. Not a shadow of blame was ever cast on the star.

Professional curiosity got the better of her. Bored, with nothing else to do, she wandered over to the mobile television unit parked some distance from the shooting site. The snub-nosed van was no bigger than Charlie's. She tried the door and found it was unlocked. Even though the van was parked in the shade, it was stuffy and hot inside. She left the sliding door open to let the fresh air in.

The interior was equipped with a monitor and a videotape player among other things. Those were the two items that interested Pet, along with the three-quarter-inch cassettes she found on top of the player. Charlie's handwriting on the labels identified the contents as part of this location's taping. She punched them into the player and adjusted the monitor screen, sitting back on the little stool to see what had been taped and what might be wrong with it.

Twice she played them through, nagged by something she knew wasn't right yet unable to fault the performer or the cameraman. The lighting was perfect and so was the background. Punching the cas-

"I've looked at those tapes fifty times. I'm taking what we've got, Pet. Let's not waste time looking at them again." Dane slid his hand across her stomach to hook her waist and attempt to draw her back to where he was sitting on the stool.

She pushed his hand away. "But I know how you can improve it." The tape had finally stopped rewinding and she could punch it up on the monitor.

"I happen to be an experienced director. Are you trying to tell me how to do my job?" There was a thin thread of anger in his incredulous question.

"Be quiet and throw your manly pride away." Pet flashed him an irritated glance. "You could listen and give me a chance to explain my idea."

"I'll listen." He sat back on the stool, folding his arms in front of him and looking anything but open-minded.

"You could give me credit for knowing a little about what I'm talking about, instead of acting so damned superior," she retorted.

His mouth twitched. "Didn't I tell you once how to shut me up if I was making you angry?"

"The problem is that you've made me too angry to do it. If I kissed you, you'd like it, then it wouldn't be a punishment," Pet reasoned in a thinly impatient tone.

Pivoting on her knees, she turned to watch the screen, which put her back to Dane. His hands closed firmly on her shoulders to draw her back to rest against his legs. Lifting the weight of her hair, he gently draped it over her shoulder.

"Then sit next to me, because that will definitely be a torment," he gently mocked. When she turned

nibbled at her lip, anxious for his reaction and certain it had to be positive.

But there was only silence that lasted through two more takes. Unable to wait any longer, Pet unconsciously swayed against him and laid a hand on his thigh, her fingers curling into the hard flesh. She was immediately the recipient of his glance.

"What do you think?" she asked.

"I think you pick the damnedest times to touch me." His eyes glinted with a wicked, dancing light before directing a glance out the open door to a crew member approaching the van. "And I think you do it deliberately." His hand closed warmly over hers and moved it to a more discreet location near his knee.

A hot wave of color flooded her cheeks, but he wouldn't let her look away from him, holding her gaze with some invisible thread. Pet was jolted by the intimacy of the moment—an intimacy that didn't rely on a kiss or a caress, but could be accomplished with a look.

"In answer to your question, you've come up with the solution," Dane admitted. "I doubt if we can achieve that pirouette shot unless Charlie is directly above her."

"We're all set up for the next number, Mr. Kingston," Rick announced, pausing at the open door of the van. "Are you coming? I'll bring the new tape Charlie wanted."

"I'll be there in a minute." He opened the storage cabinet to take out a clean cassette tape. "Here." He tossed it to the man, then began uncoiling his

# CHAPTER TEN

ATLANTIC CITY is famous for its beach and the magic of its street names—Boardwalk, Ventnor Avenue, Baltic and Oriental Avenue—familiar to every child who has played the game of Monopoly, its creator having taken the names from this city's streets. The Miss America Beauty Pageant is held at Convention Hall on the Boardwalk, which now boasts gambling casinos.

The whirring reels and clanging bells of the slot machines dominated everything. At the tables, the voices of the gamblers and dealers seemed almost muted in comparison to the din of the machines. Pet followed Charlie as he elbowed his way through the crowd of guests eager to part with their money. Coins clattered into a metal tray and a woman shouted excitedly to her husband.

"It's really something, isn't it?" Charlie shook his head.

Pet laughed at his seeming disdain. "Five minutes after you put your things in your room, you'll be down here and you know it!"

He grinned suddenly and let his hand find her elbow where the crowd thinned, enabling them to

"The place was probably too crowded for all of us to be together," Charlie offered his own explanation. "I'm surprised we're even booked into the same hotel as the casino."

"Dane probably didn't want to provide us with any excuses for being late," she shrugged.

"About the sandwich?"

"Sure, we can eat together." It was better than eating alone. "Where do you want to meet?"

The elevator stopped at his floor. "Why don't I just stop by your room in half an hour?" he suggested. "It will be easier than trying to find each other in that madhouse downstairs."

"Okay, but make it forty-five minutes. I want to wash my hair," Pet explained hurriedly, and he waved an acknowledgement before the elevator doors closed.

At the next floor Pet got off the elevator and found her room. She heard a phone ringing as she set her weekender bag down to unlock the door. Hurriedly Pet opened it, certain that the caller was Dane but the phone was silent when she stepped into the room. She wasn't even sure if it had been her phone that was ringing.

Opening her suitcase, she shook out the uncrushable dress she had brought with her, the only one, and laid it on the bed. The taupe and beige dress was simple almost to the point of plainness, with buttontab roll-up sleeves, deep side pockets and a tie belt. After more than a week of slacks and jeans, it would be a pleasant change to wear a dress, Pet decided.

She unpacked her makeup and shampoo from her

buckled the strap of her beige sandals and reached for the tie belt to knot it around her waist. At the knock on her door, she glanced at the phone. She would positively scream if Dane called her after she had gone. But how would she know if she wasn't there?

The knock sounded more impatient. Sighing, she walked to the door while making the first loop in the knot of her belt. She was adjusting the trailing ends to hang smoothly down her side as she opened the door.

"Where the hell have you been?" Dane demanded, striding inside the room and slamming the door shut. "I've been trying to reach you for the last forty-five minutes!" Pet's surprise turned to indignant shock at his raging demands that didn't permit her a reply. "I've called three times without an answer. The desk verified that you checked in more than a half hour ago. I finally called Charlie to find out where the hell you were and he told me you were on your way up here when he left you. I've been half out of my mind! Why didn't you answer the phone?"

"Why didn't you let the damned thing ring long enough to give me a chance?" she hurled back at him with equal anger. "The first time I was just walking into the room. Then I was in the shower. And then I stubbed my toe trying to get in here because I knew it was you! How dare you yell at me, you arrogant, pig-headed—"

"No." The one low word cut across her angry retort, his hard features unrelenting in their severity. "We aren't going to have another shouting match, not this time! I've waited too long."

"Of course, I've always been fully aware that you were all woman." He slid a hand down to cover her breast, letting its round contour fill his palm. "But it's an attractive sight to see you in a skirt just the same. Were you going somewhere?"

"Didn't Charlie tell you?" Pet couldn't seem to drag her eyes away from his mouth with its traces of her lipstick. Those strong male lips could create such an upheaval in her senses. "We were going to have a sandwich together."

"He's married," Dane stated.

"Yes. He's just a friend," she explained in case he wondered. "I didn't want to eat alone." Hope leaped with an eternal flame. "Are you free? I can tell Charlie—" But Dane was already shaking his head.

"No, I'm tied up this evening." He didn't volunteer any specific information as to whom he would be with or why he was wearing an evening suit and tie. "I wanted to be certain you'd arrived safely. I expected you an hour ago."

"Charlie doesn't drive as fast as you do," Pet smiled, and tried not to wonder about his plans for the evening.

His light kiss seemed to be a reward for not asking. "I want you to have dinner with me tomorrow evening, after the taping is finished. No one else. Just the two of us," he invited.

"I accept." She let her lips tease his. "On condition that you don't take me where I need to dress. This is all I brought."

"On the contrary." Dane returned the torment, rubbing his lips against hers while his fingers found

"Tomorrow," she promised, saying more with her eyes.

The two men stepped to one side to let Dane pass, then Charlie raised a questioning eyebrow. "Ready?"

"Just let me get my bag," Pet nodded, and went to retrieve it from the dresser.

Nothing was said initially about Dane's being in her room, although Lon's gaze was often half-angry when it met hers. The conversation during their meal centered on the production, with Lon filling them in on what had gone on here while they were in Batsto. After the waitress had cleared their plates and served coffee, Pet took a cigarette from her pack and bent her head to the match flame Lon offered.

"Dane sounded worried when you didn't answer your phone." Charlie finally brought up the subject that had occupied both men's minds. "Where were you?"

"Taking a shower." She didn't go into the circumstances of the other times.

"You're making a fool of yourself, Pet," Lon said irritably. "All he wants is to take you to bed."

"That's the pot calling the kettle black, isn't it?" Pet challenged, releasing a thin stream of smoke and tapping the end of the cigarette in the ashtray.

"Maybe it is." Lon reddened, but he wasn't deterred. "But it doesn't change the facts."

"And those facts are?" Her voice was as cool as her glance.

"The only way there's a future in having an affair with him is if you're sleeping with him to get some

"I appreciate the advice," she said stiffly.

He sighed. "I know you aren't going to believe this, coming from me, but I like you, Pet. I don't want to see you get hurt."

"I like you, too, Lon," was the only reply she could make.

IT WAS HECTIC getting ready for the last taping. Because another performer had given his show the night before they weren't able to set up the bulk of their equipment until the day of the taping. An hour before show time, Pet was helping Andy secure a cable that had worked loose from the adhesive strip taping it to the floor.

"Hey, Pet!" Rick called to her from the stage and motioned. "Dane wants to talk to you."

"Tell him I'll have a headset on in a few minutes."

"No. He's backstage," Rick explained.

Andy glanced at her. "Go see what he wants. I'll finish up here."

Wiping her moist palms on the hips of her brown slacks, Pet left him—but none too eagerly. Yesterday she would have raced for the chance to speak to Dane. But Lon's warning had forced her to take a long, hard look at where she was going. She didn't question anything Dane had told her or his desire for her. It was the things there hadn't been time to say— things she wasn't even sure he would have said if there had been the time. She was getting nervous about having dinner with him after the show because she knew where it would lead, and she wasn't sure anymore if that was where she wanted to go.

gagement. It wasn't necessary that he should. "I shouldn't be celebrating now anyway. My work is just beginning, editing it all together into a smooth, fast-paced show. It's just as well that we have to postpone it."

"You're always so understanding, Dane." Ruby beamed and stretched on her toes to kiss him.

"I understand that the star has a show to get ready for and she's letting me detain her." The kiss he gave back was little more than a peck. He turned her around and gave her a gentle push toward her door. "Go and make yourself beautiful."

With a husky laugh, Ruby Gale slipped into her dressing room. As Dane turned to leave, his gaze immediately fell on Pet. She started forward quickly, so he wouldn't guess she had been standing there watching and waiting, a bright smile fixed on her expression. His features gentled at her approach.

"Rick said you wanted to talk to me," she explained.

"All the time...about the silken texture of your hair, the softness of your lips, the heady warmth of your body against mine," he murmured, caressing her with his voice and his velvet dark eyes. Then he seemed to catch himself and took a deep, regretful breath. It was strange, because Pet couldn't breathe at all. "But on this occasion it was business. I want you to get some behind-the-scenes action before the show starts—dressing rooms, makeup, wardrobe, musicians, stagehands. You know the kind of color I want. And concentrate on what goes on in the wings during a performance. You should be

quickly seized on this piece of glamorous backstage color and followed him to the star's dressing room, the tape rolling.

Pet was standing some ten feet away when the door opened at the florist's knock. Luck gave her the perfect angle over the shoulder of the florist into the dressing room.

Clancy, the secretary and girl Friday to Ruby Gale, answered the door. Beyond her, Ruby Gale was sitting in front of a mirror with her back to the camera and the door, dressed in a lavender robe. The mirror's reflection gave Pet a view of the star's face. If it had all been rehearsed, it couldn't have been more perfect.

Evidently the florist had added some flattering comment of his own to the delivery of the roses, because the red-haired entertainer half turned to give him one of her sexy smiles. Her blue gaze flickered past him to the camera and Pet. She was instantly livid, coming to her feet and storming out of her room in a volcanic fury as flaming as her hair.

"You snooping little bitch!" she screamed at Pet. "What are you doing sneaking about out here?"

"I'm sorry." Pet tried to apologize and explain about the flowers, but her voice was drowned by the vicious abuse and accusations Ruby Gale hurled at her. She attempted to retreat, backing away, but she was relentlessly pursued. Too stunned by the vitriolic attack, Pet understood only half of the insults.

"What were you hoping—that I'd be half-naked so you could sell the tapes to some gutter magazine? I know how you got your job! How many men did you

shoulders and turned Ruby toward her dressing room. "Don't worry about it."

Tears scalded Pet's green eyes. She furiously blinked them away, turning to see Tom staring at her, wordless in profound sympathy. Stiff with righteous anger and raw pain, she couldn't respond to his look. She didn't need to communicate her desire to move away from the star's dressing room as Tom picked up the recorder to walk with her. Pride kept her shoulders squared and her head high, but she was trembling inside from Dane's abandonment of her. She was determined not to let it show how deeply she was hurt.

That resolve flew out of the window when Dane came in search of her a short few minutes later. A wall of stormy tears kept her from seeing him too clearly, but she had a blurred image of his tight-lipped countenance, which was all her temper needed.

"How could you let her talk to me like that?" Her angry voice scraped her throat to make the accusation hoarse. "How could you let her get away with it?"

"It's only twenty minutes before the show starts!" Dane flared. "What did you expect me to do? Try to defend you and have her do one of her exit scenes? Then where the hell would I be with all this equipment and crew and a half-finished special?"

"I don't care who she is or how important she is, nobody has a right to talk to anybody like that—not to me! Not to Tom! Not to anybody!" Pet retorted in a husky protest.

## CHAPTER ELEVEN

MOONLIGHT SILVERED the foamy caps of the waves rushing onto the sandy shore. Pet lifted her face to the ocean breeze, closing her eyes to the pain that hadn't found a release. Her hair had long ago been freed from its confining pins as if loose and falling free it would somehow allow the hurt to tumble from her. But it hadn't.

Turning parallel to the ocean, Pet began to walk again along the stretch of beach. To her left was the Boardwalk and its towering buildings and hotels etched in lights against the night sky. She didn't know how far she had walked since she had bolted from the casino theater to wander aimlessly up and down the quiet beach, avoiding the piers with their noisy rides and bright lights. She wasn't the only one walking along the oceanfront. A few others were strolling its expanses, mostly couples.

A wave came rushing in to lap the firmly packed sand near her feet, but she ignored its mild threat. Her gaze wandered ahead, studying the strip of glistening wet sand that marked the extent of the tide's encroachment onto the beach. The dark figure of a man was standing ten yards in front of her by the water's edge, but facing her and not the sea. Her

A tiny, agonized sound slipped through the constricted muscles of her throat.

He continued to tower motionless above her. "Pet, you're the only one who can buy it back for me."

The husky appeal in his voice finally pulled her head up. She searched his shadowed face. The pride and strength remained forever carved into his features, but his dark eyes were haunted.

"When the show was over and I found out you'd walked out, I didn't try to find you right away. I went back to the control van and sat there, going over in my mind what had happened and what you'd said." Turning, Dane sat down on the sand beside her, adopting her position and letting handfuls of sand run through his fingers. "I thought I had the thing that was most important to me right there in front of me—the show tapes. Not in so many words, but you told me what an arrogant, selfish bastard I was. I've been called that before, but coming from you...." He sighed heavily and clasped his hands between his spread knees, studying his linked fingers. "What I'm trying to say, Pet, is that what's important to me is your love and respect. Nothing else means anything."

"You don't really mean that, Dane," she whispered sadly. "You just want me to forgive you so you'll feel better. You don't care whether or not I love you. We haven't even known each other long enough to fall in love."

"Maybe you haven't, but I've been waiting for you all my life." His gaze locked onto hers and refused to let it go. "I love you, Pet. I realized it the morning

"Why not?" Now he was watching her, his gaze searching through every nuance of her expressions.

"Because...all that work...all that time...." It was impossible to think of all the reasons when there were so many. "You've spent a lot of money."

"A lot of money," Dane agreed. "But it's worth every dime if you finally believe me."

"I believe you." After that kind of sacrifice, how could she doubt him?

"Do you forgive me?"

"Of course," Pet breathed, just beginning to realize the fulfillment this meant. "Dane, I fell in love with you, too. I was the most wretched person in the world when I thought the man I loved could care so little about me that—"

But she was never allowed to complete the sentence as his hand reached to pull her off balance and into his arms. He was kissing her and murmuring love words that she would cherish in her heart forever.

When Dane finally allowed her to surface from his loving assault, she was lying on the sand, her head pillowed on his sinewy forearm while he leaned partially over her. She drank in the sight of his compelling face above hers, passionately ardent in its expression.

"When will you marry me?" he demanded.

An old fear returned. "Do you really think I can keep you happy?" she whispered with a catch in her voice.

"No one else can. Haven't you accepted that yet?" he mocked. "No one else can irritate me and goad me into an argument quicker than you can. No one else

beach? After all your lectures, Dane Kingston, what will people think if they see me?''

"Dammit, Pet!" He started to get angry, then laughed. "I have champagne chilling in my room." He kissed her hard. "And if you dare say a lady wouldn't go to a man's hotel room, I'll strangle you!"

She linked her fingers around his neck and gazed at him impishly. "Who ever said I was a lady?"

# Choose from this great selection of exciting Harlequin Presents editions